Venice

The Sigh of the Bridges

Paul Beccaria

Translated from the original French by Regina Rhodes

Cover :
"Amare Venezia" Acquerello di Monica Martin
www.itacaartstudio.com
info@itacaartstudio.com
© Monica Martin – Itaca Art Studio, Venezia, Italia.

ISBN : 978-2-9563102-6-6

EAN : 9782956310266

October 2019.

Special Thanks

An enormous thank you to Marjorie without whom this novel would have never come to fruition. Marjorie has brought an incalculable contribution to the creation of this work; she was an ideal collaborator from the start right up to the end.

I love and admire her infinitely.

4

To my daughters,

"The world is a wonderful book, but it is of very little use to those who don't know how to read it"

Carlo Goldoni,

Born in Venice February 25, 1707, and died in Paris in 1793

Preface

Certain bridges listen to the gondoliers sing.

Others make music with the lapping of the water, stirred by the boats.

Bridges smile while children play at hopping on their steps.

There are some that grumble when they are awakened from their sleep by party-goers.

And also, mischievous bridges who whistle at young women in a rush to meet with their lovers.

And then those which remain as inanimate as marble before so much beauty.

And those of granite who would love to be made of wood, while those made of wood want nothing more than to be of stone to no longer be padlocked by those who promise to never leave one another.

And finally, there is this bridge, which was perhaps enchanted by its creator, or simply gifted with the power to inspire the dreamy-eyed painters.

Go to Venice. Find your bridge. Make a wish and hope it comes to fruition before leaving this town, or you won't have a choice but to come back.

VENICE

The Sigh of the Bridges

I

It had been now more than an hour that Dave had been sitting on a bench, just there, at Champs-de-Mars only a few yards from the Eiffel Tower. Before him, the Iron Lady, proud of her three hundred meters of height, remains composed in the face of hordes of tourists come to admire her and artists who set up shop daily to paint her likeness.

That day, he was there, notebook and pencil in hand, ready to sink his teeth into her. The Eiffel tower would be his last subject before leaving the capital. He had recreated most of the monuments of Paris over the course of his exchange semester spent at the *"Ecole Nationale Supérieure des Beaux-Arts",* or the National School of Fine Arts. A little smile grew from the corner of his mouth when he thought to himself that he had finally reached the end of his studies at the Institute of Fine Arts in New York, but he would no sooner revisit its buildings as he had found a source of creativity elsewhere while meandering in the name artistic pilgrimage. Sitting on the little bench of an all-too- 'Parisien café' where he went in to buy cigarettes, was his inspiration, and she was called Lisa. From that moment, they began sharing a studio and within two weeks they left for Italy. The two had planned to spend two months in Venice before their definitive move to Rome to allow Lisa to take her first job and then join the worksites of Trastevere. Two weeks. The time necessary for her to support her thesis in archeology, and for him to paint the Eiffel Tower. It was all so deliciously cliche. To fall in love with a French girl who was half English, just as brilliant as she is beautiful, to go paint in Venice while following the footsteps of the greats, and then to Rome with her arms reaching out to him. He would have never predicted all this while the wheels of his suitcase were wedged between the ramp and the gate while boarding his flight to Paris. He smiled ever-so-slightly at the memory. He could not concentrate on the tower; he really could not do it. His mind, his thoughts, vanished into thin air and were carried off in a gust of emotions. A mixture of melancholy in thinking of the wondrous moments spent on the streets, in the bars and in the sheets of Paris, and of the excitement regarding all of the beauty which awaited him; yes, he was decidedly incapable of concentrating.

He also thought of the museums overflowing with canvases of the greats, of the Italian Renaissance, Michaelangelo, Leonardo di Vinci, Raphael, of the cathedrals and their extraordinary ceilings, all of the art history which swayed and danced in disorder in his mind. A new wave of inspiration awaited him there, he was sure of it. But for the moment, sitting on this bench, he stared at the tower of iron, his gaze already far away. He knew with absolute certainty that this page would remain blank, in waiting.

"I ran into Nervani today."

"What's Umberto got to say?"

"He confirmed that everything is ready for our arrival in Rome. I went back and forth with him to get him to understand that we're postponing until September, in the end he got that we wanted to enjoy Venice a bit before leaving. Anyway, it's all worked out."

Lisa printed out the documents while trying to organize and stack a veritable disarray of papers of all sizes, states, and colors.

"Awesome, in any case, I booked the apartment up until the end of July, so it's for the best!"

With a playful air, he slinks behind her.

"Well Madame *almost* Doctor of old rocks, how does it feel to almost be finished with all of this?"

"You're kidding, it's *far* from being finished! Come on, help me out and staple these lists of erratum instead of distracting me!"

"Come on, just one little minute…"

"That's really not flattering yourself"

"Oh, you know exactly what I meant, you can finish after… I could not even paint today I was too excited...by all of this, the plans. And I thought about you…"

He pulled her close to him and kissed her neck.

"I've got direct orders from your personal doctor; your prescription is the best therapeutic sedative there is."

**

The driver of the taxi boat placed the last suitcase at the foot of the stairs leading to their apartment. Dave had called the real estate agency to organize the hand-off of the keys once they had arrived. It was already the end of the afternoon and Lisa had one goal in mind: to take a cold shower or a bath. It's a guilt-ridden thought for all those who've just arrived in the Venetian Republic for the first time, but man's self-esteem is reduced considerably when his most basic needs are left unsatisfied. So, one can only marvel at such beauty. Lisa had decidedly passed the stage where she could reason or rationalize her irrepressible desire to escape this heat which had been overwhelming her for the entirety of the journey turning her into an only slightly more lively wet rag. At this moment, bathing had become an absolute necessity.

They had just left Paris the day before, driving in the Citroen Berlingo that Dave had purchased upon arrival in France. That valiant steed had charged through the Alps without hazard before leading them all the way to Torino where Dave and Lisa took a break. However, the next morning, halfway between Torino and Venice, the car literally collapsed. At least its motor had. Lisa, while waiting for the tow truck underneath that unforgiving sun, watched her thoughts transform into an amorphous mass of incoherent reflections. There is a little oddly shaped candy in the south of France called a Berlingo. Why would they give a car, such a utilitarian object, a name like that? While they both had a similar geometric shape, and were relatively hideous, it had absolutely nothing else in common with the candy for which it was named which was actually named after Clement the Fifth, his real name being Bertrand of Goth which became Berlingot. Eventually she began to fear she would share a similar fate, under the blazing sun, her and the Berlingo candy were destined to melt. Valiant steed, they had called it, a term she knew no longer applied.

Just after Milano, a road sign reminded Lisa that the old city of Bergamo was worth the detour to make a little visit. Dave, too rushed to get to Venice, preferred to continue, arguing that they would have all the time in the world to double back for the visit during their time in Italy. But Candy, a name they now used ironically to refer to their mess of a car, was of Lisa's opinion, and stopped suddenly in front of Bergamo's airport. Lisa might have laughed from the irony of it all if Dave had not seemed so tense after calling his insurance company. When the tow truck finally arrived after an hour of waiting on the side of the road burnt by the sun, the diagnosis was incontestable: Candy's motor had essentially melted and Lisa whose interior laughter had unfolded into the pure delirium one experiences before a mirage in a desert, was severely sunburned. The trip to the mechanic shop took place in the tow truck itself, which was of course without air conditioning. Amidst all the noise and hubbub inside the truck and across Lisa's newly sullen face, Dave was babbling on about how the man who sold him the car had guaranteed that in spite of the hundred and forty thousand kilometers shown on the odometer, the car could still push through another hundred thousand. Through his babbling he also kept an eye out for sympathetic looks from Lisa's direction and alternated his gaze toward the driver with his incredibly basic and awkward Italian diction as the driver nodded mechanically, his mind elsewhere as he calculated how much he would profit from this little interaction.

At the shop, the mechanic abandoned the idea of repairing the car in favor of a simple certificate of destruction. The adventure with the Berlingo was over, Candy was gone, leaving in its place an awfully bitter taste.

A taxi was sent to bring Dave and Lisa to Venice. The transfer of the onslaught of suitcases and baggage took place yet again under the overwhelming heat of the sun and it was not until they were settled in, car doors closed, inside the air-conditioned taxi on their way to Venice that Lisa's mood began to brighten. Dave, unshaken, was sitting in the passenger side next to the driver trying to perfect his Italian and turning back to look at Lisa where the conversation might have concerned her. Lisa felt better, but not better enough to enter the social game of discussing anything and everything with perfect strangers just to avoid the silence. Her skirt, which had been taken by shock by the cold of the air-conditioned car, had not yet had the time to dry from their sweaty trip in the tow truck and was now sticking stubbornly to the leather of the car seat. That was enough to render anyone asocial.

While crossing the Liberty Bridge, the long entryway into Venice, Dave was still talking about his car, finishing by saying that it was just as well because he had not even thought about the problem of parking his car in Venice for the duration of their stay and perhaps the cost of leaving the car in a paid lot would have been about the same as the price he paid for the Berlingo in the first place the outcome was bittersweet Afterall. He was not able to successfully translate this last part into Italian based on the look he was given out of the corner of the driver's eye, or maybe the look was just meant to signify his weariness after Dave's word vomit and a hopefulness that it would soon stop.

The taxi turned in the direction of Tronchetto, where the taxi boat mandated by the insurance company was meant to wait for them. The driver parked, unloaded the suitcases on the dock before the empty pier and then left the couple there, promising that the boat would be arriving soon. It was not until the taxi was already long gone that Dave finally shut up.

Lisa sat on one of the suitcases, gazing vaguely into the void. Any semblance of human form she had rediscovered in the refrigerated taxi was now completely lost, and she melted once again into her liquid form within minutes. A half hour later, it was a newly tense Dave who called his insurance company yet again who guaranteed that his request had been registered and that they would call the taxi boat to see how the situation was progressing. Without fail. It was the use of the word "*situation*" that made Dave doubtful that things were actually moving along, and when the agent called him back to tell him that the taxi boat would be there any moment, that moment turned into another half hour. Once the boat finally reached the pier, Lisa had been completely transformed into a syrupy puddle. However, it was just at this moment that she felt a light breeze from the lagoon and once again filled with the mad idea that she would one day be able to use the shower in the apartment that awaited them on the other side.

**

The employee from the real estate agency arrived in front of the apartment at the same time as the couple. Having warned her about their tardiness, Dave and the agent were able to synchronize to hand-off the keys. One last effort to take all the suitcases up to the second floor and Lisa was rushing into the bathroom, shedding the thin layers of fabric which had begun to form a second layer of skin. Dave finished bringing all the bags into the bedroom with a look of satisfaction. After all, it was not so bad, he even got the chance to practice his Italian in a real, authentic situation.

He stepped on what must have been a skirt just that morning, and he wanted to laugh, but he held back. It was a better idea to wait until Lisa was under the stream of the shower before trying to joke about anything. He pitied the poor girl, and he was mad at himself for not having been able to create a more romantic arrival in Venice. When it was all over, it would make for an interesting story that they would be able to laugh about but not until well after the shower had worked its magic. He picked up the skirt and tried mechanically to shake out the wrinkles, but his efforts were in vain, the garment was completely worn out after the voyage. He threw it even further, not really knowing what to do with the thing and thought delightfully about the body off of which it had just been peeled. He followed the path lined by the other discarded articles of clothing which led to the shower, undressed, and joined Lisa to see if the shower's charms were at work.

**

The weight of the air made it almost impossible to breathe, and it was not even July yet! It led one to believe that the summer was going to be incredibly hot, even if Lisa could not really be certain considering she had never spent a summer in Venice before. But she was sure of one thing; they were going to suffocate in this city soon to be swarmed with tourists. She needed air.

Lisa went down to the terrace of a café not far from their apartment and ordered a fresh-pressed juice. Dave was supposed to join her to go and visit museums that they had not seen in the past few days since their arrival. Lisa had, of course, made a list of all of them and was determined to cross all of them off before their departure.

The server brought her drink and did not seem to be too busy. Lisa saw the opportunity to have a conversation with a real Venetian, and she seized it. She started out by talking about the heat and then about the magnificence of the monuments in the city, all in her hesitant Italian which was insufficient to express the full extent of what she wanted to describe but was decent enough for the server to smile and play the game without resorting to a response in English. He was a tall young man with brown hair that raged above a playful regard and a strong nose with a slight curve.

"The heat really is suffocating today; we'd be so much better at the beach."

"At the beach?" Lisa almost stuttered on the word. "How do you expect to get to the beach? Unless you mean you're going to lay down on the pier and roll yourself into the canal!"

"I suppose that's an option! Personally, I would prefer to hop on a little motorboat and go to the sandy beaches of Lido."

"There's a beach in Venice?"

"Of course! The first of the Adriatic Sea. Where are you from? You're French, aren't you? And you come to Venice without even knowing what there is to do here?" He responded in a playful tone.

"You guessed right! But I stopped at a few at the North Sea, the English Channel and the Mediterranean! No, I really didn't realize that there were beaches in Venice."

"If you would like, I have a break from 5 to 7 this evening, I can take you there."

Lisa, surprised by the proposition, was going to mumble a response right as Dave approached and took a seat next to her. The server asked what he would like to drink, and he ordered a beer.

"I'll bring that out to you right away, sir."

He disappeared into the café.

"Am I hallucinating or was he trying some Italian courtship just now?"

"No. I mean, yes, but it was good intentioned."

"Oh, I'm sure it was!"

"Oh, c'mon! He offered to take me to Lido beach. Did you know there were beaches in Venice?"

"Hmph. You sure that was not just a terrible pick-up line? Beaches in Venice? Where? Between the lagoon and the buildings?

The server came back whistling with the beer on a tray.

"Here you go sir, a nice cold beer."

"Thank you," responded Lisa, "to return to our conversation, we're staying in Venice for a while and the heat has me shut up inside. I've just been alternating between our apartment and the museums. Or café terraces. Anyway, I was wondering if it would be better to sit inside your bar, maybe it's cooler in there."

"Oh, no ma'am, here you're in the shade and downwind of a nice breeze rolling in off the lagoon. You two have a lot fresher air here than inside, our air conditioning is broken."

"I see. I was just saying to Dave that you had proposed to take me to the beach. But he does not believe there could possibly be any sandy beaches in Venice."

The young man smiled without getting flustered.

"Of course, there are! And we have the most beautiful beaches in the world. Well, nearly, after the beaches of Seychelles.

"Well, would you look at that! That's Italian chauvinism, I guess," laughed Lisa.

"You'll see what I'm talking about, they truly are the most beautiful, I guarantee it. At 5 this evening, meet me here, both of you and I'll take you there. It only takes about twenty minutes to get there by motorboat."

**

The days that follow seem to pass at the speed and exact rhythm of a cruise ship: in the fresh morning air Dave and Lisa visited museums together and took advantage of the moment of exploration to stake out locations where Dave would like to paint. As the morning ended and noon rolled around, the pair took a motorboat over to Lido to eat salads in a restaurant and then idle around in the sun. They went back as the afternoon came to an end to remove the salt and get cleaned up before heading back out to shop around or stock up on groceries for that night's meal.

This sort of routine did not last long, however, and Lisa thought back with nostalgia to her first moments in Venice, though the nostalgia was punctuated with moments of bitterness. She saw for the second time the moment when Dave told her to go to the beach in Lido alone. He had preferred to go back and paint and said they would see each other later in the evening, she should go ahead and enjoy the beach without him. He left her there, on the dock before the motorboat, her purse in hand and she alternated between a desire to laugh and a desperate need to ask what had happened which caused him to change his mind so suddenly. She managed to stammer out that she would go back with him, but she understood clearly that he just wanted to go back alone to get started on his work. Once she was laid out in the sun, she felt stupid for having experienced that moment as a sort of abandonment. She had no reason to feel that way. After all, he had come here specifically for that reason, and he had every right to want to paint that day. However, that bitter feeling remained attached firmly to the memory, maybe because of the way everything had happened. Too quickly, too brusquely, too radically.

And she was not wrong. Their rhythm had radically changed. Once Lisa came back from the beach, Dave was not in the apartment. She went to pick up some groceries and made something to eat, and she was still alone in the apartment. It was not until late after the sun had set that Dave came back, only to get a better start at dawn.

Painting! It's all that's left in his mind. He only has eyes for this city. And heaven forbid I mention that I'm actually still here, a living breathing part of the Venetian backdrop, because then he might actually *see* me! Lisa despaired over the whole situation and could not wait to get to Rome, she hoped she would be able to break what seemed to be a curse once they arrived there. She was afraid of the silences that began to settle. The silences which she filled over the lengthy days with often bitter thoughts. Thoughts which crept in between her and Dave, even when they were together.

**

The whole month of June poured out at the same unchangeable pace. Dave painted and just as soon, Lisa left to the beach, to revisit the islands of Murano and Burano. There she could talk with the artisans who did stunning work with glass, or with the lace workers who sewed lace tirelessly. How beautiful they were, hunched over their work, with their ear to ear smiles the instant one took the time to stop and talk with them and share a moment of their lives. Lisa was now speaking much better Italian and every day her conversations with the Venetians grew more and more interesting.

There was only one dark cloud hanging overhead and shading this painting, her painting; Dave was completely absent from her days. He passed his most illuminated moments outside, painting, and the only moments where their paths crossed were during the nights and some meals spent exchanging only pleasantries, hardly speaking. Deep down, her frustration was bubbling and mixing with her inability to tell him what she truly felt. She felt guilty to feel deserted, but a part of her was screaming that she was well within her right to want to live together and share their lives and not simply coexist as housemates. Her emotions would get too mixed up to the point of her being unable to untangle them and formulate expressive sentences over dinner, and she just preferred to go to bed, lulling herself to sleep with the idea that tomorrow, spontaneously, things would take a turn for the better. However, nothing changed, it was just her interior anger which dulled out to eventually, calmly, transform into destiny. Their relationship eroded and seemed to only leave behind a carapace, devoid of life. She did not recognize how much she was lying to herself by thinking that this would pass, by holding on to a daily life completely devoid of purpose.

**

A warm wind came in from the open sea. The freshness of the evening lasted only a second. Lisa was beginning to understand the moods of the local weather and could determine with certainty that the day was going to be much hotter than the ones before. She came down from the apartment. Dave left early, as he normally did, leaving her to face another Venetian day alone. She decided to go out and get some air, and she stopped on the way at a bar just below her place to get a coffee.

"Hello, Madame!" The server said to her, "What a lovely tan! Can I assume that you've taken a liking to my beach?"

"Yes. Well, Lido beach because as far as I can tell there is not any sign indicating that it's a private beach belonging to Mr. Prince of Venice." She gently mocked him.

"And your prince, he is not with you?"

"No, my boyfriend is a painter. He's in some Venetian labyrinth! He spends most of his time there."

The barman was surprised by the harshness in Lisa's voice.

"He should be careful, it's easy to lose a fiancé in Venice's maze!"

She did not respond. He continued in a cheerful tone.

22

"Come on! Smile! What can I give you in exchange for a little smile?"

"A coffee please. That should wake me up, I did not sleep well. It's just too hot!"

"I can do better than a coffee. The beach is not mine, I'll admit it, but I have a little skiff to myself. How about a little stroll along the city's canals? Private tour with an authentic Venetian!"

Lisa hesitated a moment, then she thought about the day and how she would have to spend it alone yet again, and about the heat. A little stroll would certainly help her clear her head.

"Venetian, sure. But 'guide', we'll have to wait and see! Okay, I'm in, but you're not working?"

"I finish in ten minutes, and I don't have to be back until noon, it's your lucky day!"

They crossed the little plaza near the café and approached the canal where the little skiff was moored. He was the first to jump down onto the pier, which swayed a bit at first as though it were about to flip over.

"Come on, you next little lady. Don't be nervous, I'll catch you."

"Firstly, let's stop with all the *ma'am* and *little lady*, my name is Lisa. And secondly, I'm not nervous!"

"Yet another reason to jump, then. And you can call me Enzo, Prince of the Seas!"

Lisa placed a first foot in the boat and rocked a little too far forward, Enzo caught her and took advantage of that moment to hold her. Lisa pushed him away quickly but gently and sat on the plank which served as a seat. Enzo was wearing his satisfied smile and set the motor en route, directing the skiff on the canal. Ten minutes of complete silence had passed before Enzo spoke again.

"On your right, you can see the house of Marco Polo. The Great Adventurer!" He said it in the voice of an international tour guide and in a much more accented and musical Italian.

Lisa smiled. Regardless of the awkwardness she forced herself to think of it as awkward that she felt once she had fallen into Enzo's arms, she felt relaxed and natural with him. The late morning stroll already seemed promising.

**

Back at the bar, the church bells rang out twelve times, announcing that it was noon. The morning has passed, and Lisa had not realized it, lulled by the movements of the little boat cruising along the canal.

Enzo helped her out of the boat and proposed a drink to finish off the morning with a Venetian apéritif.

"Oh, come on! Just a little spritzer! Before I start my shift. You're not going to slip away so easily."

"I'm not slipping away. The little trip was wonderful and you're a great tour guide, and I want to thank you for this morning at the canal. But I still have museums to see and a book to finish."

"Okay, well either you have a drink with me, then you go and get your book and I give you the best seat in the house, or you can have lunch here and read as much as you want."

"You've got a lot of nerve! Who told you that I wanted to spend my whole afternoon here?"

"Just a feeling. Come on, it's my treat. You can do whatever you want afterwards, but not before you've tried our special: a salad with fried seafood."

She looked at him, hesitating. He was like a child, giddy about a surprise yet to come. She did not see why she should refuse him given the day she had ahead of her. The unexpected company permitted her to break free from her solitary routine, and she could still do exactly what she'd planned to do after. Her curiosity, tinged with greed, took over.

"I accept the offer, but I refuse to let you treat me, I'll pay my own tab. I would be too uncomfortable, and in any case your boss will ask questions."

"My boss! It's my uncle, and he's kind of exploiting me anyway, so he just lets me do more or less what I please. As long as I work on Sundays, I can treat whoever I want."

After the apéritif and the meal, the afternoon passed pretty quickly. Sitting in the shade of the alcove, Lisa was deep into a work which detailed Byzantine archeology. It was Enzo, whose voice rang through, reminding her that she had not moved for the whole afternoon.

"I'm all done, and you?"

"Done with what?" She asked.

"My shift! I'm free. Am I taking you to see a museum now?"

"Authentic Venetian guide and museum guide on top of that, who would have guessed!"

"I'm going to take you to see a museum where you would never think to go on your own, and somewhere your painter would never take you."

"Oh my! Should I start getting worried? Is it a museum on the ocean floor that requires submarine transport? Or is it in the cosmos, will we be on the next NASA craft?"

Enzo laughed, a good-hearted laugh, and responded while smiling.

"Even better. It's here in Venice, in the neighborhood of San Marco, and we'll get there in ten minutes on foot."

"You're full of mystery!"

"Trust me, you won't be disappointed!"

Lisa gave him a smile, took her bag and they left in the direction of the infamous plaza.

**

Once she got back to the apartment, Dave was already home. It was late and the whole day had gotten away from her. Enzo showed her Venice from the inside, the true and authentic Venice, and she was completely under its charm. And to top it off, Enzo had the ability to make her laugh, there was a constant little pinch reminding her that she had not had this much fun in a long time. She was tense at the sight of Dave being at the apartment before her, it was a bad coincidence, but it made her feel nonetheless guilty for missing a moment with Dave which would have otherwise been spent painting in solitude. But, after all, she had nothing to blame herself for, she could not be expected to simply wait around the house all day on the off chance that he would come home a bit earlier than normal. The 50s were over and long passed, thank God! Women had taken control of their liberty and she certainly counted on keeping hers.

"You're back late," were his first words.

She bit her tongue to hold back from responding that for once it was her and not him coming back the latest, they were far from being on equal terms, but she did not want to let her bitterness take over, so she restrained herself. She took on a cheerful air to choke back the bile.

"I was with Enzo. I bumped into him at the café and since I was not really doing much, he took me to visit a museum, it was particular but pretty interesting nonetheless."

"Oh! What makes it so much more special than the museums we've already seen together?"

"It was the museum of eroticism."

"Ah, okay! Did you participate as well?"

"And there you go, straight to that! Do you always have to have your mind in the gutter?"

"Please don't try and convince me that this guy is not trying to woo you! As a matter of fact, maybe you're interested in him too."

"Of course, I find him interesting, but not in the way that you're implying! We had a very 'typical' day in Venice, that's it! He knows the city well, and he made me try out some local specialties, it was really delicious. You should."

"So, it's exactly what I said, my mind is not in the gutter and I'm not imagining things: the guy is pulling out all the stops for you!"

"Just let me finish! Can I finish talking first?! You're not understanding anything that I'm saying to you!"

"Quite the contrary Lisa, I understand very well."

"No, you don't understand anything that's going on! Be honest with yourself, Dave. For you, there's nothing aside from painting! You don't seem to understand that I need you here with me, you're *never* with me. What do we share, huh, these past few days? Sleeping? Enzo makes me laugh, for example. How long has it been since we laughed together? You don't even realize it but you're completely isolating yourself, and you're excluding me. Enzo offered me a bit of friendship and you're seeing it as adultery! It's pathetic that you can't even see the difference. But you know what, I don't need to justify myself to you, I haven't done anything wrong."

Lisa finished her sentence, her voice heavy with sobs. Dave looked at her, saying nothing he stood up and left, slamming the door behind him.

Riddled with pure anger, Lisa went to bed. She hated him; she was mad at him for causing that scene. She thought she was the one who should be jealous of him, of the fact that he was always out painting. Eventually she calmed down and tried to listen for noise in the room next door to see if he was there, but he was gone. She turned to face the empty side of the bed and placed her hand on the sheets, hoping he would come back to lay down next to her.

At the crack of dawn, the space was still empty. Dave had not come back. She got up and went into the main room of the apartment, the couch was also empty. Only the marks of a man who had spent the night on it remained. Dave had come back late and left early as he always had, this time with one difference: the one thing that they had shared before the bed, his side was too cold to bear in the summer heat.

Lisa wandered from alleyway to alleyway, lost in her thoughts. She just could not make up her mind to cut off contact with him, and she was determined to bring up the subject of their depart for Rome. She remembered the night before, after their umpteenth argument, that he had grumbled the name of a bridge where he painted, between the neighborhoods of San Marco and Castello, and she thought a neutral place outside of the apartment might be more fitting for the conversation. After a quick glance at the map she always kept in her pocket, she took a chance with random streets meant to lead toward those neighborhoods in the hopes of crossing paths with him somewhere around one of their bridges.

"Don't move!" she stopped, immediately. She had just walked onto the bridge when she saw him sitting there behind his canvas. He had also seen her, magnificent with the sunlight shining through her hair and creating arabesques in different patterned sections of her dress. He had to make her part of his painting, she understood this without him even having to vocalize the idea a simple gesture of the paintbrush, and she obeyed, hoping that this little moment of complicity would revive the connection between them.

She leaned over and placed her elbows on the side of the bridge, facing the canal which stretched out toward the next bridge, only a few meters away. He said nothing to her and plunged back into his work behind the canvas, painting rapidly while maintaining precision.

The stones of the bridge had been darkened by time, a phenomenon which the past century's pollution had only exacerbated. There were ornate reliefs depicting animals and various shells adorning the arch of the bridge. She was trying to make out the friezes surrounding the reliefs, they were composed of a variety of symbols and geometric forms. On the ridges of the pontoon she could make out something engraved on the decorative border, but it was so ancient that she was unable to discern if they were letters, numbers or simply more designs meant to be purely ornamental.

She kept staring at the engravings and tried to give them some sort of sense or signification. Her background in archeology took over and the curiosity to decipher the inscriptions became an obsession. She thought she saw characters which looked like Latin, or rather Greek, or perhaps Hebrew, everything was a blur. When Dave finished his sketch, he offered nothing more than a simple "Okay". She took a moment to try and retain the images of the symbols in her mind before going to join him. He thanked her and there was a smile shared between them, creating at least for the moment a sort of complicity that they had not experienced in a long while.

The day was approaching its end, and they went back to the studio together. That evening there was no fighting, everything was calm. Lisa shared the discovery she made while on the bridge earlier. Dave had been painting for several days in that neighbourhood, and yet he'd never really noticed the inscriptions, and he did not think he had seen anymore elsewhere for that matter. After dinner, they did what all lovers do. Lisa could not get a precise date from Dave for their depart to Rome, but he promised that it would be before the end of the week. The next morning, she felt surer of herself and decided to go to the Marciana library in San Marco's plaza to do some research. Perhaps she would be able to find some more information about that bridge, some older and clearer photos or some details about the language in which the inscriptions had been made in the stone.

**

Since that night when he had promised they would be leaving for Rome before the end of the week, another week had come and gone. Dave had once again taken up his rhythm of leaving early and coming back late. He avoided conversations with her that went on for too long and risked veering toward the subject of them leaving for Rome. Now, it was very clear to her that any mention of Rome would evoke the same reaction in Dave: he would turn his gaze to a more neutral corner of the room, shrug his shoulders, and mumble in an irritated tone something like "I don't know" or "soon", both of which actually meant "never". She was convinced, he had fallen for the charms of Venice and could not be shaken out of it! She felt a constant and terrible sense of selfishness. Did she truly love this man who preferred his art much to the detriment of their relationship and the sense of trust, and without regard for her own desires?

She knew that work could monopolize any situation, it's not like she did not understand that this city had an immediate hold over people, even her. But this reflection did not help her feel any less resentful.

At least she still had the engravings from the bridge, the enigma they represented was enough to occupy her curious mind and to help change her thoughts.

She had already thumbed through the navigation registers, military reports and several other books relating commercial exchanges from the past centuries. For the most part, they retraced a part of the history of Venice over the course of the years. It was an entire slice of history into which she had never delved. The librarian who had explained everything to her the first time and to whom she addressed all of her questions was an affable man in spite of a slightly abrasive external, which she felt was well suited for someone in charge of conserving precious knowledge. Up until now he was pretty good about giving her direction in her research, even though it remained more or less fruitless. For once, she was not under any time constraints on her quest for information, so she allowed herself to get lost searching for unrelated historical accounts of the city itself.

This is exactly how she spent several afternoons, taking advantage of the coolness of the library, entrancing herself with tales of conquest, of gold and of masks outlining the history of Venice. It was while consulting one of the arsenal's registers brought to her attention by the librarian that she discovered something of interest relating to the bridge's engravings. The arsenal had acted as a military building, but at the moment of its construction in the twelfth century, it served as a naval building site. On a page dedicated to the lions that guarded the entryway to the arsenal, it was noted that there was an engraving on the back of one of those marble lions. The next page showed a rather detailed reproduction of the engraving. The letters looked, without a shadow of a doubt, like those she had seen on arch of the bridge. In the footnotes, it was mentioned that Scandinavian mercenaries had engraved these words on the lion, the fruit of their victory on their return from Athens. They had left the lion in Venice, along with plenty of other ornamental rocks, drapery, jewelry and other precious objects, all in exchange for gold which was easier to transport on their journey home. She was overwhelmed by a feeling of satisfaction. All she had to do now was to inform herself about the symbols used by these people. She knew it would not be a simple task, but the joy she got in thinking about this new adventure was fresh and almost childlike; deciphering this new code would make her feel like the heroine of some great adventure novel. She laughed internally, imagining herself in an Indiana Jones movie, the one cliché which followed archeologists to every dinner, every conversation or any other situation requiring one to respond to the question, "And you, what line of work are you in?".

She left the echoing silence of the building to call Brian Tolls, the only one who could set her in the right direction quickly. Brian, an eminent archeology professor, was her co director and advisor in the thesis writing process in London. He had always been a great source of support for her through the years of research, constantly encouraging her during difficult moments, always helping her get back in the saddle when it seemed she had reached an impasse.

Once the surprise had passed, it was replaced by questions regarding her satisfaction in her new position in Rome. She squeezed out a rushed response, explaining that she would not be starting until September to get back to the purpose of her call. He gave her the contact information of a colleague who was a specialist at Oxford. After some warm "thank you", she hung up and called the new number immediately.

The professor answered almost as soon as she rang. He did not take long to respond to her request, he listened to the descriptions Lisa gave him, asking a few questions just to be sure and was able to confirm that she was, in fact, looking at runic writing. He also took the time to explain to her that around 6,500 different dialects had been discovered across the continent of Europe, and even though they were used since the 2nd century, most of them had been lost over the course of history and had never been translated. He could not tell her the meaning of what she had described to him, but if she sent a copy, he could let her know as soon as they could make sense of it. She expected nothing less, knowing from firsthand experience the curiosity of researchers, she thanked him and ended the call.

All she had to do now was wait. The adventure was over! She could go back to the beach.

It was already late and in spite of the feeling of satisfaction she got from the productivity of advancing in her work, she knew she had to go back and re-shelf all of the books before the library closed.

She took the pile of documents and registers and got started in one of the aisles on replacing the items methodically. When leaving a section to advance to the next row, she ran into a man who was holding a book in his hand. The crash was not anything violent, but it was enough to destabilize her and send the leaning tower of Pisa formed by the books she held in her arms crashing to the ground. The man immediately asked if she was okay, but she responded that he was standing in the way and he made her drop everything.

Sure, that he held no guilt, but more interested in helping the beautiful young woman before him than reprimanding her for her accusation, he apologized out of courtesy and began helping her pick up the piles of books. She mumbled a "thank you" before scurrying off quickly.

It was only once she was in front of the row of books, incapable of remembering if the H came before or after the J that she realized she was trying to recall the scene and recreate the man's face from memory. She smiled internally at the ridiculousness of it all, and went back to arranging the books, trying to calm her mind with a well-ordered alphabet.

**

It was Sunday morning. The streets and alleyways of the neighborhood were still asleep. Dave was arranging his things inside of a bag, drowning in an outpouring of terrible coffee. Lisa, eyes still shut, listened to the noises of the apartment. It was Sunday, and Dave continued to disregard any thought or conversation regarding their departure to Rome. There were the sounds of a zipper, sounds she knew all too well-meant that Dave would finish his diluted coffee while packing his painting bag as he did each of the mornings preceding this one. He would put on his shoes, almost fall, grumble to himself and hold onto the wall for stability with a hollow thump noise, and then exit in a flurry of jingling keys and the grinding of the door handle. He would not be back until much later today, and he would only respond to the rare question with short and irritated quips. His newfound mutism was akin to a sort of hypnosis which rendered him completely inaccessible. She did not recognize him anymore. She started to wonder if she had ever really known him, if their life in Paris had actually existed. Each night, under the false pretext of fatigue, she isolated herself in the bedroom to avoid him. That was what their relationship had come to. That was who they were now. Even in the stories her friends confided to her incessantly about their not-so-successful love lives, there was never anything this pathetic. At least, with the others, there was conflict and resolution, awkward attempts at conversation, but never this distance, this feeling of living with a complete stranger to whom you have nothing left to say. She was trying to dismiss the feeling, but she realized the utopian nature of the goal they had set for themselves, and she could have sworn their decision to go to Rome was made together; at that time they were still talking and she swore that it was him who pushed her to accept the position when she was wavering for fear of making a selfish choice and imposing this move on Dave when he had no desire to go. But this feeling never left, nor did the thought of Rome, further and further away seeming every day less and less capable of providing the two with a new start. Nothing would shake Dave from his sickening apathy. He had no intention of going to Rome, this much was clear. And she was not ready to sacrifice everything for a phantom that existed only in her memory.

It was Sunday. He was gone. Like every other morning, she had to get up and leave to keep her mind busy and chase away the anxieties that left only when she escaped those four walls. But this morning, maybe because it was Sunday, maybe because she needed to breathe in some new air, perhaps because she could feel her dreams escaping her and dissipating in the Venetian alleyways, or maybe because it was simply the moment, she did not get ready to head to the beach, or to a museum just to pass the time in the day. She got up, showered quickly, took her suitcase from the wardrobe, threw her clothes inside haphazardly, and then checked the schedule for trains heading toward Rome. She took the time to scribble out a short message for Dave, and she finally felt herself again as the rhythm of the train's movement enveloped her.

**

George left the library. The critically thinking part of his mind was mocking him for the deviation of his thoughts, which alternated between an adolescent need to replay the meeting with this beautiful young woman, and the summary of his research from that day. At 32 years old he found himself imagining all the possible dialogues they could have had if she had not rebuffed him, if he would had used something else as bait for conversation, and he felt pathetic. He was not there to meet his soulmate, a concept which he had already stopped believing in a year ago when Anna announced the night before their depart for Milano that she would not be coming with him, that she would be staying in London, that it was better this way. She did it all with an almost respectable calm, she was poised and had clearly spent time reflecting on the matter. No, he was not there to try to woo any Italian women and certainly not any Italian-speaking Englishwomen. He was on a mission for the Research Institute of Milano in the ISAM (Institute of Studies on the Ancient Mediterranean), he was an investigator of Roman civilizations on a quest for decisive elements to finalize a study on the impact of the construction of navigable roads and paths by Romans throughout Europe. Quite a mouthful. He did have to admit that she was damned beautiful though, the stranger, and the situation, something pulled straight from a Hollywood classic, lent itself to dreaming.

He smiled at his own childishness and then headed towards Harry's Bar. The spritzer he was about to order would be well-deserved before going back to Milano the following morning.

**

The line 1 motorboat showed up at the dock where George awaited his transfer to the parking lot for the past few minutes. There were only a few scattered tourists remaining, the last stragglers of the horde who had come to run through the backstreets of the city during the summer, just to snap some photos and then hurry back to the same jam-packed motorboat. Then, after a short wait at the train station, they went straight back to their daily lives. George smiled at the thought and then boarded the little boat.

"Ferrovia"

The intercom on the boat announced the stop at the Sainte Lucie station.

George always felt a bit of nostalgia as he passed this stop before arriving at the Piazzale Roma parking lot and heading back to Milano. But his stay this time was very productive, and he was excited to get back and apply the fruits of his research as soon as possible.

Standing near the exit, lost in his thoughts, something or someone bumped into him.

"Hey!"

He felt someone pulling on the strap of the bag he held in his hand, and they were pulling it in the direction of the exit gangway. It was not as though he had not been constantly warned. He, just like everyone else, had memorized the posters cautioning passengers against pickpockets after reading them time after time while waiting in train stations, and he had listened to the intercom announcements reminding boat passengers to remain vigilant, the same robotic voice which serenaded everyone else who was trying to tune it out. He pulled on his bag, and noticed that the strap was stuck in the handle of a rolling suitcase, he pulled again but the closure could not stand up to all the force and it gave in, spilling out a colorful mass of clothing onto the ground.

The person on the other end of the suitcase handle stopped short and turned around. Their face changed from an expression of surprise to one of anger. George immediately recognized those two expressions which he had already provoked on this exact same face: it was the young woman from the library. He did not even have time to feel sorry before she accosted him for his lack of attentiveness, his stupidity, his awkwardness, saying that he had screwed everything up and she was going to miss her train, and that he was good-for-nothing, and that he had better help her pick everything up off the floor instead of standing there staring at her like a dead fish, and that he was just bad luck, and that...

George remained frozen before this outpouring of words, incapable of getting a word in edgewise to excuse himself and explain that it was a terrible coincidence. He was fascinated by this ball of anger. He knew that if he took her into his arms that she would dissolve into tears, but he changed his mind, not wanting to damage the pride of this stranger who seemed oddly familiar in her turmoil.

Eventually he became more reactive and removed his hand from the suitcase, just in time to avoid getting his fingers snapped up in the zipper as she closed it. He did not even have the time to help her pick up the suitcase because she had already done it in the blink of an eye, turned around and rushed toward the station.

George sat on a bench before the docks. His motorboat had already left, and the intercom had announced that the next one would be arriving in fifteen minutes. He thought back to the distress of the young woman. He was mad at himself for not having reacted more quickly, but the virulence of her emotions had completely frozen him, or rather fascinated, even though he thought the term rather unfitting given the nature of the situation.

He was still lingering on this moment in his thoughts when he heard a woman crying behind him, he did not even need to turn around to know that it was her again. The walls had finally caved in. He got up and walked slowly in her direction, giving her time to see him and react if she did not want him coming any nearer, which she did not do. Instead, she crumbled up a letter she had in her hand and quickly shoved it into the pocket of her cardigan.

"I'm sorry about earlier… I didn't react, you were so angry, I mean, I could have helped you and I'm sorry. And I'm assuming you missed your train because of all this. Listen, I'm waiting for the next motorboat to pick up my car from a parking lot and head to Milano. Is there any chance I can drop you off somewhere to make up for what's happened?

She had calmed down somewhat while he was speaking to her. He was wondering to himself if he should have just stopped talking to be sure that she would not start back up crying again but she surprised him with what seemed to be the start of a smile.

"I'm the one who's sorry for everything that I said. It wasn't your fault. It's just that lately nothing seems to go according to plan, and it's pretty difficult to digest. Your bag was just the straw that broke the camel's back."

"I don't want to be too invasive and ask for more details, but I insist on apologizing for my part in your distress. Can I drop you off somewhere?"

"I'm leaving for Rome, but I do have a transfer in Milano. I guess if I don't want to miss it, I have to take you up on that offer."

"I'll get you there in time! I promise to make amends."

She dabbed her eyes and stood up.

"My name is Lisa Wood."

"George Bennet. It's a pleasure to meet you, a second time."

She smiled.

**

Dave was on the boat approaching the station. Still far from the dock, he spotted Lisa sitting on her suitcase, crumbling a letter before stuffing it in her pocket, standing up and leaving. Not alone, no, the silhouette of a man materialized in Dave's retina suddenly, a man he had not noticed until that moment. That was it then. It was not just a simple desire to move on to Rome, it was to go to Rome with someone else. It was obvious now that he thought about it. Of course, she had met someone else while he was painting, he had been too busy painting, now that he had finally found his inspiration and rhythm, the light and the stroke of the brush, it was real and it was what he had waited for, for so long. And she had gone and met someone else, probably in a bar, but that was not important, she was leaving for Rome with another man, who certainly was not him.

He felt surprisingly calm when he got off the boat to take the one leaving in the direction from whence, he came. Calm, but full of spitefulness. But she did not understand the importance of his art, she did not see how important his engagement to his painting was, that he had a duty to respond to his inspiration, and she could have just waited, he would have just needed a bit more time.

**

It took George two hours to get to Milano on the highway. Lisa, sitting next to him, had quickly begun to feel at ease next to the natural calm of George. The discussion brought them to talk about their professional lives and both were shocked to learn that they shared a residency in London at some point. Lisa had carried out a portion of her studies there and George was born and raised there up until the end of his academic career. He went back regularly to visit, the mother company of the association that had hired him after his internship had its main base in London.

The habit of exchanging stories between colleagues quickly did away with any reservations that Lisa may have had left. All the same, concerning her reason for coming to the City of Doges, she remained evasive, she did not want to have to talk about Dave. So, she responded with a quick summary:

"I came with a friend I made toward the end of my studies; we were roommates in Paris. I really needed to take a break before starting my career, and Venice seemed perfect to start my discovery of Italy."

"I understand," responded George. "I had the same feeling after my internship. London is a great city, but to relax, I preferred to opt for a week in Paris."

"Paris?! We could have bumped into each other. Well, actually, no, it's better off that we didn't. You might have gotten stuck on my suitcase!"

"Oh, you're feeling sure of yourself!"

42

"I'm only kidding! I still feel guilty, I'm sorry to have dragged you into my problems.

"Don't worry about it, I am a little responsible and I'm happy it happened with you and not someone else, it's more pleasant this way. If that same thing would have happened with a Venetian, they would have sent me packing, it wouldn't have been pretty."

Lisa had picked up on the flattery, but she did not comment on it. She had not missed out on the fact that George was a charming man, she was far from indifferent about this after having stolen a prolonged glance in his direction while he was focused on the road. But given her last experience, she scolded herself. She was going to Rome, alone.

"But the Venetians are so nice!"

"Yeah, they're super charming! As long as you don't get in their way! They seem at least equally as rushed as Londoners!"

George's car arrived in front of the train station in Milano. George walked with Lisa to the ticket sales counter, carrying her suitcase. Lisa tapped at the reservation screen to buy her ticket. The screen reflected back: SOLD OUT

"Oh, NO! This is just what I needed. I'm really going to start thinking that I'm cursed or something."

"Look for the next one."

"That was the last express train. I'm going to have to take the regular one that stops in every single town. It's going to take hours!"

Lisa went back to the home screen and started a new search for regional trains. On the screen was written:

Next departure:

DUE TO TECHNICAL DIFFICULTIES THE NEXT OUTBOUND TRAIN WILL BE LEAVING AT 11pm

"No, no. Just, no! That's not possible. What in the name of God have I done to deserve this?"

"Let's calm down," George said with a little smile and plenty of compassion. "God has nothing to do with it, it's the train company that's got it out for you. The train for Rome won't get you there until dawn. You won't be able to sleep on the train with just those little cushions and all the noise. Just take that first express train in the morning. I'll drive you back to the station, and in the meantime, I can take you on a tour of Milano by night!"

"Oh, no. I can't accept that."

"Oh, come on! Don't start turning me down again. Be realistic, the night train is a real nightmare!"

She bit her lip. She had already experienced the misfortune of travelling on the night train once and still shuddered at the memory. After all the emotions of the day, she did not really feel up to a red-eye train ride.

"Okay, you're right, but drop me off at a hotel."

"No, I insist. Let's grab dinner in a restaurant near my place, it's a modest little bistro but they have an excellent chef. The food there is just divine. And then you can sleep at my place, I have a guest bedroom that hasn't been used since I moved in. I promise, I will not try anything. It's just late and I know that the hotels in Milano are going to see you show

44

up without a reservation and they'll charge you a fortune. Say YES, you have had more than enough problems for the day, let me invite you out to atone for my part."

Lisa hesitated for a brief moment, but the kindness and the charm of George won over.

"Okay, I'm in, that's really kind of you. I don't have any fight left in me; all this has completely exhausted me. And an empty stomach isn't really helping the situation, I could go for a good plate of spaghetti!"

At the restaurant, Lisa devoured a plate of Milanese pasta without saying a single word and drank the Barolo wine up until the moment that dessert was served when she finally got a hold of herself and said:

"That pasta was absolutely divine, and the wine was a clever accomplice to lead me right into dessert, but I'm stuffed. Really, thank you, George."

"The pleasure is all mine. I'm happy that you accepted to stay and dine with me."

Their gaze remained fixed upon one another for a few seconds before George, realizing the situation, said:

"Will you take a dessert? They're all delicious."

"No, thank you, I want to finish on the good taste of this wine."

"The bottle is empty, should I order another one?"

"No, that won't be necessary, I already went a little overboard."

George and Lisa headed back to the apartment with a light buzz from the Barolo wine a lover's vintage. Lisa would not be on the train to Rome the next day, but while climbing the stairs pressed into George's arms, she already knew that.

II

At Harry's Bar, Dave was leaning on the counter as he had done every other night for the past few weeks. He felt at home among the crowd of strangers. This bar had a reputation for sheltering artists of all sorts. However, he was not here to socialize. He was looking for people, the noise, the frenzy of the lives of the unfazed, at least on the surface. Just to feel surrounded, to once again be among others.

Something had changed since Lisa left. He felt it. It was working away deep inside him. He felt it in his paintings. He realized that he was going for new shades to work with, darker, and his paint strokes had changed as well, more ethereal maybe, he could not really say. In some ways, he was happy about it. He felt like what he was painting made sense. That was the only thing left anyway, that had any sort of sense. That and the moments he spent in Harry's Bar.

**

Dave arrived at the bar a little early. He was not happy with what he had painted that day. He knew that such is the lot of the creative process, these inevitable hollow moments. However, this time it seemed like something different, something more profound. As if something had cracked inside of him, a simple fissure, but it was certainly there. And then there was this cold, a chill, that had come over him in the middle of the afternoon and he had not been able to shake it. He had come to see if the chill was caused by a wind whistling through the alleys or if it was emanating from within, lodged in his innards. His first indicator, a whiskey with no ice, was insufficient to respond to his questions. He was already on his second, having dived deep into his pessimistic thoughts, when a man came and sat next to him on a barstool. He addressed the barman:

"A Milano-Torino, please."

"Sorry sir, I don't think I understood. A Milano-Torino?"

"Yes, yes. A Milano-Torino."

"Sorry, but I don't know that cocktail."

Dave, momentarily pulled out of his thoughts, felt obligated to intervene.

"He wants an Americano, actually. It's an Americano, a Milano-Torino."

"Oh, yes of course! Excuse me, I'll get that for you right now," responded the barman. "Thank you, sir" he addressed to Dave.

"You're very welcome."

He turned to his new neighbor.

"You aren't from around here. In Venice, we just order Americano, that's the generic name."

"Ha! I'm such a novice!" George responded warmly. "I wanted to change from the same old whiskey and look what happens, I seem like some yokels come to rub elbows in a bar for the first time. I'm a historian, actually, and I felt it was sort of a professional obligation to try that cocktail, but I only know outdated name apparently. George Bennet, pleasure to meet you."

"Dave Burnside."

"Thanks again for the bar etiquette lesson."

"It's no problem."

"Are you American, Dave?"

"I sure am! And you're English I suppose?"

"Ah yes, our accents precede us!" said George.

"But yours is much cleaner than mine is. I really work at it, but there are just certain sounds that don't want to come out how they should."

"Well, you know, I'm cheating, I've been living in Milano for a few years already, I've got ample opportunity to practice. Do you live in Venice?"

"Yes and no."

After having explained his geographic journey, Dave finished:

"So, technically speaking I live here, but I don't think I'll be staying. I was supposed to leave for Rome, but I changed my plans."

"Oh, yes. Changes in plans! That's the primary motivation in everyone's lives I believe. I'm here to do some research, I actually come pretty often. I came to have a drink and not stay shut up alone in my hotel room. I like Venice at night. Without the tourists, the city is so beautiful."

"Yes, she is magnificent, that's why I stayed. For her."

"Worse than any woman!"

"You said it." responded Dave bitterly.

The bartender placed the Americano in front of George.

"Thank you! So, a toast to the women of Venice!"

He took his first sip of the cocktail without noticing that Dave had not raised his glass.

"It's delicious, thankfully you were here, I would have missed out in this! So, you paint?"

"Yes."

"I'm fascinated by people who create. Personally, I've got no talents!"

"Everything and anything can be learned. And I'm sure you have talents in other areas."

"Oh, I certainly do!" George responded, laughing. "I can confidently say I'm good at what I do. And when someone has to dig up a source of information, you can be sure that it's me they call, especially if the information seems impossible to find!"

"It's funny, while painting, I found a bridge with an inscription on it. Bit by bit I started doing research about it, but I still can't figure out what it means. It's a language that I don't know, and let's be honest I don't know much. And all the languages that I found don't match up. I think I'm at an impasse."

"That's the exact moment when my colleagues contact me, systematically, to ask me to launch an investigation and find a response."

"What a funny coincidence."

"Isn't it? I guess now I'm going to have to help you."

"Oh no, that's not why I mentioned it." Dave responded, slightly embarrassed.

"I know. But to be completely honest, I'm naturally very curious and I wouldn't forgive myself if I passed up on an opportunity to resolve a mystery."

"Professional obligation, again?"

"That's it! Everyone's got their poison."

"There are a lot worse!"

"That's true. I know some ancient languages, hopefully one of them is what we're looking for. Otherwise, I can help direct you in your research. If you can remember these inscriptions, maybe you can describe them for me."

"Well, no, unfortunately I don't really remember them, and I don't have a photo on me."

"Oh, Oh! Well, what a shame."

"But if you're not doing much else tonight, you're more than welcome to come and have dinner at my place this evening. I don't have much in my refrigerator, but I can cook up some pasta dishes pretty well." Offered Dave.

"That's an offer I can't refuse!"

"We'll keep each other company this evening; you seem to need it as much as I do!"

"Are you saying that because of the cocktail situation?"

"No, it's more so my empty whiskey glass that's calling out for another."

"So, let's go then, you're going to need to have your wits about you to follow my rants and ravings of a mad historian throughout the evening."

Dave laughed frankly at the response of his companion in misfortune. He certainly needed the company to help change his ideas for the evening. And even though it meant taking advantage of the work Lisa had already done, he still hoped to solve the enigma. He developed an interest in the symbols that he had drawn and doodled mindlessly so many times before. It was an enigma that held something mysterious at its core which interested him, he had dreamed about them again the night before. In the dream he stood before the bridge and let loose a phrase that seemed improbably long relative to the number of symbols in the inscription, and the bridge began to tremble. The water reached its boiling point and blocks of stone began to fall in, eventually he was enveloped in water. When he awoke, he was drenched as though he had really fallen into the water. He knew it was nothing more than a bad dream brought about by the two whiskeys he had knocked back in the place of an actual meal. But that was yesterday. And, against all expectations, this evening was off to a better start.

George paid their drinks, then they left, heading in the direction of Dave's apartment.

**

Not far from them, a short man with a weather, beaten face and greying hair, was sitting before his glass of beer. Like any other patron of the bar, he had come after work to partake in happy hour. But, turned toward the counter, he had listened to the conversation of the two men as discreetly as possible. Once Dave began talking about his discovery, he got up and went to sit at the counter with his beer. He shuffled around in the bowl and pulled out handful after handful of salted peanuts, and to justify him changing seats he began to address the bartender using a Venetian dialect.

"Hey! Gotta be American to get something to nibble on around here, huh?"

It was a rhetorical question to which the barman was far too busy drying glasses to be bothered to answer.

The man tossed a few peanuts in his mouth, then a mouthful, all while listening to the men's conversation. A few minutes later, he stood up and followed them down the street.

**

"It's on this."

Dave pulled a sketch out of his pocket and held it out to George.

"Can you see, the inscriptions there, on the side of the bridge. And here," he indicated, "I drew them larger."

"Are you absolutely sure of what you've drawn, no errors, no mistakes or omissions?"

"No, I'm completely certain that I've copied everything exactly as it was."

"Very well. It's certainly an ancient language. We can guess the structure of the phrasing, here, have a look, the order of the symbols is canonical, but obviously not our canon."

"You already lost me there!"

"Ha! You'll have to excuse me, I'm just accustomed to talking with my colleagues, it's bad manners on my part! I'll look at all of this more closely and I will contact you from Milano as soon as I know more if that works for you."

"Yes, that'll work. Here, something to take notes on."

The pasta dish was not exceptional, but the wine continued to loosen their tongues. The two men spent the evening talking about anything and everything. Dave seemed to be avoiding subjects that were too personal, and George, understanding, quickly stopped asking questions that may have made him ill at ease. He had only gleaned that the painter arrived in Venice with a woman who had since left him. He could feel that the subject was still a sore spot, and he diffused a potentially frustrating situation by sharing his story of being dumped. Without any formality or ritual, just before a planned departure for Milano; this girl that he was dating for the past year just sent a message saying she did not feel like going with him, and she preferred to stay in London.

"Infamous English apathy!"

The two laughed heartily about their 'misadventures', and clinked glasses to the soft weakness of men.

The evening dragged on a bit and then George took leave of his host, promising that they would meet again during his next visit to Venice to share another drink.

On the landing of the stairs, George stopped a moment to make sure that he had not forgotten anything at Dave's place. When he raised his eyes, it seemed to him that a shadow was turning the corner up ahead. He wondered to himself who would be hanging out in the streets at this time on a weeknight, and then reminded himself that this is exactly what he was doing. He laughed to himself, thinking he had probably had too much to drink, and then returned to his hotel.

**

After his meeting the next morning, George made up his mind to make the most of the last few hours he had before leaving Venice to go to the library one last time. He knew there were innumerable books and archives which mentioned, even if it was indirect, a number of ancient languages. That could always be helpful to narrow down his research on the symbols he had taken down in his notes the night before. He knew by heart the sections which were dedicated to antique languages, but for the information he was looking for, he knew he would absolutely have to ask the librarian for some direction. The grizzled librarian pointed him in the direction of the appropriate aisle, warning that he would not find any texts specific to the subject concerned, but he could start some cross-referencing to help.

George headed toward the stacks where he started his meticulous research, one pile of texts after another.

**

Behind his desk, Aldo Vitelli, the librarian, had his mouth pinched shut. He was staring mindlessly at a notebook and wondering if he should say something or not regarding this coincidence. Two people looking for information on the same subject within the space of a few months. His memory had never failed him, even though he had never had to use it for this particular reason.

He picked the phone up from the receiver and composed the number he had memorized by heart.

"Hello, Mr. Scalla? I think I might have something for you. Come quickly."

**

An hour later, George found a book inside of which were images of symbols quite similar to the ones found on the bridge. It was a Celtic language from a region in the Great North. The work itself dealt with the maritime and terrestrial flow of the Vikings and the period during which they had invaded Venice. They had left behind statues and monuments for the Venetian patrimony, many of which have since disappeared or had been destroyed after being judged as 'useless' to the grand public.

He took notes on the more pertinent passages to later be able to, or at least make an attempt to translate the inscriptions upon his arrival in Milano. This would give him a good foundation to begin. He decided to stop here, replace all of the archives and materials on their respective shelves, and then thank the librarian before leaving toward the parking lot.

**

Back in the research area, a man put down the newspaper that he had been flipping through distractedly up until that moment.

He stood up, made a very discreet gesture in the direction of the librarian and traced the same path as George.

He followed him, all while making sure to maintain a certain distance between the two of them. When they arrived at the parking lot, he went ahead of George to pay for the parking before standing off to the side pretending to rearrange some receipts in his wallet, to allow George to pay his. When George inserted his ticket into the machine, the man made sure to get a look at the section in which he was parked and in order to be the first to arrive in proximity to

George's vehicle, he made his way to the elevator. He crossed the elevator's threshold as quickly as possible to hide himself behind a cement pillar and wait for George to arrive.

Once George exited the elevator, the man, now hooded to hide his face from the security cameras, jumped out of his hiding place to stop him in his tracks. However, at exactly that moment, an errant tourist appeared, seemingly from nowhere, to ask George about where the security office was for this floor because she needed to get her keys back from the valet. George offered that they walk together because he, too, needed to go and pick up his keys. The man, having been interrupted, watched the two of them walk up to the security kiosk and then headed off toward his own car.

George's car left the lot, followed by another. They had set off in the direction of the Liberty Bridge in Milano.

**

It was already night when George finally arrived in Milano. The city had been emptied of its traffic jams and now, calm, the nocturnal illuminations made the city shine. He parked his car on the street in front of his building where Lisa was surely waiting. She was certainly already home for the weekend.

George had only walked a few steps when he felt a shoulder knock into him from behind, causing him to lose balance and almost fall if he had not caught himself by leaning on a parked car. While he was trying to regain his balance, the stranger ripped his briefcase away from him and took off running. Dazed by the rapidity of the attack, he remained frozen where he stood on the sidewalk without making a sound. He lingered for a moment, immobile, then he began to laugh. He laughed at his foolishness, the misunderstanding, the weariness, and the disappointment. It was all so silly. It was not like he had lost anything of actual value, he kept all of his important papers in the inner breast pocket of his blazer, and in truth the briefcase only had documents from work which he could easily print off a second time. The incongruous nature of the situation. The schism between his impatience to get home and the violence of a situation he felt was odd considering the location and the time. Yes, it was certainly a form of violence. Even if he was not physically affected, it was still a destabilizing event.

He took a few steps in the direction of the entrance to their building and then, realizing he left his suitcase on the pavement, doubled back to grab it before returning to the entrance, dragging his feet as though sleepwalking.

**

Giovanni Scalla stopped running after a few blocks, passing two additional apartment buildings. He fell back to a walking speed and headed nonchalantly to the first restaurant on his path. While he was waiting for his pizza, he placed the briefcase on the table and opened it to verify its contents. Inside were some pieces of paper and a notebook. He began to read it and did not stop until the server came with his coffee. He had not found anything of interest. Frustrated by the time wasted, he paid the bill, retraced his footsteps back toward George's building, got in his car and headed back to Venice.

**

At the threshold, George paused for a moment to gather himself in order to show a calm face when greeting

Lisa. He did not want to bring his misfortune into the house and spread it around. Finally, he entered their apartment, sinking his keys into a glass bowl from Murano which brightened up the entryway considerably. He uttered a greeting in a tone which was louder than normal to make himself heard by Lisa, wherever she might be in the apartment.

She was in the kitchen, cleaning up what was left on the table after having cooked.

"Good evening sweetie," she responded after George had already walked into the kitchen. "You seem tense, did you have a bad day?"

He could not keep anything from her.

"No, no, the afternoon in Venice was rather pleasant."

"Oh, really? It's just that you seem a little upset, it's the tone of your voice. And normally when you walk through that door and greet me, there's a little magic word attached," she added, mischievously.

"Nothing gets past you, Madame Detective! Actually, something weird did just happen to me downstairs. I was attacked by some guy who stole me briefcase."

Lisa, pale, stopped her cleaning.

"And are you okay? Did he hurt you?"

"No, no, at least not physically. It's just frustrating to be shaken up like a fruit tree and then robbed in the middle of the street like pickpockets used to. It's the 21st century for god's sake!"

"I guess some things never change... And as for their motivation...maybe they were hoping to find your wallet, or they're planning to resell the briefcase and make some money off of it. Do you want an aspirin?"

"No, thank you, I think I'll have a whiskey before eating. That should calm me down. Thank you honey!"

Lisa smiles and kisses him.

A newspaper in his hands and an empty coffee cup placed on the table before him, Giovanni Scalla had been sitting there for an hour. With the only point of entry or exit of Dave's apartment building in his direct line of vision, he waited for Dave to leave. He had been trailing Dave for two days now and had been able to track all of his movements, the times of his comings and goings. It was now just a question of time before Dave would be leaving the building to get started on his painting.

The church bell rang out ten times. Dave appeared, his work materials tucked under his arm, and headed off in the direction of the town's center. Scalla stood up as soon as he saw Dave leave and walked toward the apartment. His back against the door, he looked around to check for witnesses and then picked the lock with little hassle. He climbed the stairs to the second floor and opened the door to the apartment the same way he had opened the entryway downstairs. As soon as he entered, he heard a voice coming from the other side of the home.

"Is that you Mr. Dave? Did you forget something?"

It was surely the cleaning lady. Before getting a response, she had already appeared in the entryway. He was not prepared for this.

"Who are you? What are you doing here?" She yelled.

She hesitated between running straight at him with her broom in hand and approaching the telephone on the hallway table. Scalla did not give her the time to decide and disappeared behind the door.

III

At eight in the evening, George buzzed at Dave's door. He was passing through Padova and decided to take advantage of the moment to stop in Venice to show Dave the fruits of his research.

"Yeah?" Crackled the intercom on the buzzer.

"Good evening, it's me George!"

"It's open."

Dave unlocked the door to the entryway.

"You need to pull it closed, and hard. There was a break-in this week. Come on up, I can tell you all about it."

George was at the doormat in front of Dave's apartment. The door was half open and Dave was calling from inside.

"Come on in! The door downstairs has to stay closed because of the other renters in the building who heard about the guy that got in. He did not steal anything, but he bumped into the lady who comes to clean the common areas. She was at my place. I give her a few extra bucks to help maintain order in my apartment once a week. She's from the East, and she's a mountain of a woman. She came across him, and he must have freaked out seeing her brandish that broom, so he left without getting whatever he came for. But you can imagine how alarmed my neighbors feel now."

"Well," started George, "at least one of them didn't get what he came for. It wasn't the case for the guy who attacked me! Last time we saw each other, I should have left with your housekeeper!"

"What do you mean? You were attacked in Venice or do you have a thing for Slavic women?"

"Ha! No... Well yes, can you believe that I got robbed on the street when I got back to Milano? And no, I'm not attracted to your housekeeper, it's just that if she had been with me, she could have knocked the guy out with her broom, and I wouldn't have had to go and buy a new briefcase."

"He took your briefcase. I hope you didn't have anything too important or valuable inside that thing."

"No, it's the case itself that was valuable, well, more sentimental."

"Well, it's not too bad then, all things considered."

"That's true."

"Come on, I'll serve you a stiff drink, then we'll eat, and you can show me everything."

"Sounds like a plan!"

Once Dave had served the after-dinner drinks, George began to show the results of his research. He spread out on the table all of the notes, sketches and translations he had done. George tried to reorganize it all, but he was only able to reassemble a bit from the beginning:

"Dreams and thoughts can be brought to life when spoken aloud or..."

Dave seemed fascinated. The translation could have multiple meanings, George explained that it might not be in the appropriate order. The sentence was still pretty obscure, but it could have been the handiwork of the pieceworkers who created the bridge, having written Celtic curses to ward off enemies, or the motto of a mentorship, or just a random superstition.

George had oriented his research in this direction and had been able to find passages from the Bible which echoed the translations he made. The passages also had commentary from 12th century monks which reappropriated and explained the citations from the two prophets.

"From the Bible! Didn't you say it was runic or something like that?"

"You know, beliefs are often found to be shared from one civilization to another, to make a long story short. So, it really isn't that shocking to find a local superstition adapted into sacred texts whether directly or otherwise." George responded.

He handed him copies of two texts.

"Then the Lord told me: "I will give you my message in the form of a vision. Write it clearly enough to be read at a glance. For the vision is yet for an appointed time, but at the end it shall speak, and not lie though it tarry, wait for it; because it will surely come, it will not tarry."

"For I know the plans I have for you," declares the Lord, "plans to prosper you and not to harm you, plans to give you hope and a future."

The writings which followed, meant to clear up or explain, at least in part, the sacred texts were even more obscure and left Dave scratching his head for a long moment. George observed him during his confusion and decided to leave him the time to absorb all of the information. He was captivated by what he was reading, and finally he offered a rough explanation.

"That could mean that the thoughts become reality when they're spoken aloud on the bridge."

George was stuck on the opinion of the monks and responded to Dave.

"Maybe, but according to the hazy explanation of the monks, it would seem as though by announcing one's thoughts and dreams out loud every day that they become reality, just on the strength of conviction. But all of that is a bit far-fetched. They're nothing more than beliefs dating more than a thousand years back. Thinking about something doesn't *make* it happen, if that were the case everyone would know it. It's great for dreamers, but when we want something, we have to act in order to obtain it".

**

The entire night, Dave thought back to that translation, the words, and the citations. George was far too *rational* about the whole thing. All of this was so unclear and yet he seemed so sure of his translation, that nothing was missing to help elucidate and understand the text. Dave was determined to find the detail which escaped him.

First, he searched through all the canvasses he had painted relating to the bridge, then he took out the documents given to him by George. He looked over again and again the totality which was dispersed over tables and chairs before deciding to go back to the bridge itself. Maybe he had left something there, he had to be sure. As he approached, he etched out each stair, step by step until he arrived at the point on the bridge with the engravings. He looked for the missing detail, scrutinizing each stone of the bridge, observing the shapes, colors, marks left by time or use. It was not until the end of the morning that he spotted on the upper right side of the bridge a stone of the same size as those with inscriptions, though the color was different. It was light grey while all the others were slightly less weather-worn. It was not in the alignment with the other stones which formed the phrase, but rather part of the base. He walked around the canal, to the other side in order to see it more closely. He could tell that the stone had been moved, probably during construction to restore the bridge. He thought that if it was placed correctly, it might have the last bit of the phrase on it and give the whole thing some order or sense. He decided to come back after nightfall with some supplies to pull it free and get a closer look at it.

Toward midnight, the neighborhood was deserted. Equipped with a painter's knife and wooden scissors, the only tools available to him in his artist's kit, he went to pick out the mortar surrounding the stone. It was much quicker and easier than he had imagined, the mortar from that time period was apparently not very resistant and time had contributed to wear it away. The stone moved, he twisted it out and turned it over to reveal three symbols identical to the ones which constituted the phrase on the inscription. He took note of them and then replaced the stone with some colored paste he found in his workshop; he did the job hastily to cover up his meddling.

**

Back in his apartment, he could not sleep, he was in such a rush to complete the phrase with his newly acquired information.

He paced back and forth in the room, whispering repeatedly the words translated from the inscription, searching all corners of his mind to try and put things in order or give them some sense, a signification. His eyes darted back and forth between his completed canvasses and the rapid eye motion made it so that the paintings melted into a sort of black wave, undulating along the walls. He felt as though he was drowning in these dark waters. He felt anxious, he stopped, rushed to the telephone and called George.

The call rang through to the machine.

"Hello, this is George. Please leave a message and I will call you back."

"No, No! I don't want to leave a message. I want to talk to George!"

He threw the phone and it landed on the couch, he grabbed the bottle resting on the chest and after ripping out the cork, he took a gulp.

"At least you're here with me."

He brought the bottle to his lips again. A few minutes later, after finding his calm again, Dave went back to his reflections.

George had left him with all the files from his research and the translation of other texts which had allowed him to translate the inscription. He used all of this and after two hours of digging through all of the documents, he had extracted the two words:

"LOST FOREVER."

Meaning that the entire phrase may have gone as follows:

"Dreams and thoughts can be brought to life when spoken aloud or lost forever."

Now completed, the phrase finally found its sense in Dave's eyes. A multitude of thoughts invaded his mind, all entangled with one another. One thing was clear, he absolutely had to go back to the bridge and pronounce this phrase. He left into the night.

The sleeping town contrasted with Dave's agitation. Standing firmly in the middle of the bridge, out of breath, he opened his mouth and spoke the inscription with a shocking clarity that resonated into the night. Everything became blurry, as though he were looking through a cloud. He felt as though he was losing consciousness and then suddenly the fog cleared, and he was in front of his apartment building, suitcases in hand. Lisa was next to him and the two climbed the stairs leading to the apartment where they would be staying for the duration of their time in Venice. It was hot and Lisa had left to shower, the door barely closed. He brought in the rest of the bags and could not wait to join Lisa in the shower to refresh himself. When he opened the bathroom door, the room was empty.

**

Lying on the bed, the sound of the bells awoke him. His head was hurting. He remembered the night before, the bridge of reflection, his vision, what he experienced again with Lisa. Was it all a dream, a hallucination, or had that actually happened? It had to be real. He was sure that the bridge was enchanted and that it would give him an opportunity to start over at zero with Lisa. He just had to tweak certain details. He had to choose the right moment to revisit, the one that had changed everything between Lisa and him. But which moment? He took a minute to think, and he remembered the moment when Lisa left to take the motorboat to the train station. She arrived at the pier around five that evening meaning that she had left the apartment around four o'clock. It was then, at that exact moment that he needed to be home to intercept and apologize for never being around, to tell her that he loved her and that he was finally ready to leave for Rome together. But, how would he do that? The response came into his mind and shone through with absolute clarity: he needed to be on that bridge at four in the afternoon.

At the expected time, Dave was on the bridge of reflection. He thought back with intensity to the moment when Lisa left, and he read the inscription again. The same fog surrounded him, and he found himself transported three months into the past at four in the afternoon in front of his building. As quickly as he could, he ran up the stairs, he burst through the door and into the living room only to find it empty. Lisa was not there; he checked the bedroom in vain. Lisa had left the apartment already. The feeling of disappointment set in and he felt as though he were falling into a void.

A door slammed shut in the building's hallway. Dave jerked awake. He was back in his bed and the migraine was there with him as well.

Two hours later, after having eaten breakfast, he washed it down with a coffee that helped him regain some semblance of reflecting capability, Dave realized that it would be nearly impossible to determine the exact moment when Lisa left the apartment. He couldn't allow himself to continue fumbling around aimlessly. Every experiment left him with headaches which were intensifying each time, and it seemed like it took him longer to come to his senses the second time.

In spite of it all, he knew he had to try at least one more temporal excursion. He wrote a letter to Lisa, asking her to wait, saying that he would leave with her, asking her not to take the train, that he had finally understood that it was her whom he wanted to spend his life with and lastly, that he would be on the next motorboat to join her at the station. He went back, once more, to the bridge of reflection, he thought back to that morning when he left to go and paint while Lisa was still sleeping. He read the inscription on the bridge and found himself again in his studio at the threshold at dawn. Lisa was asleep. He slid the letter in her pocket and left.

When he opened his eyes, he felt as though his head was going to explode. The room was spinning around him. He wanted to stand, but all around him was flowing water from the canal which began to replace the floor in his room, and his bed was floating in harmony with the canal heading toward the bridge. He passed out. Once he came to, he was covered in sweat. Alone, in his bed, his was still threatening to explode.

The phrase echoed in his mind.

"Dreams and thoughts can be brought to life", it had failed him.

In spite of his efforts, Lisa had tossed the letter at the entrance of the train station.

**

The time passed and Dave faded away. The departure of Lisa, his failed attempts to get her back, all of it began to weigh upon until he felt himself entering into a slump where he splashed about sinking further by the minute. His thoughts were unclear, all entangling with one another, mixing desires, his past and his fantasies. When he got up, it was to paint with the shutters half-open. The light horrified him and seemed to burn his retinas. It wasn't until he had gulped down his first few glasses of whiskey that he began to feel a sort of life come back into him. He had started smoking again, bit by bit, and eventually everything in his apartment had been turned into an ashtray. When the cleaning lady came, she lectured him constantly.

"You smoke too much! You need to air out the room! What a mess! Listen, Mr. Dave, you have to do something. And all the bottles, this is unreal!"

But, what could he do? He was alone, and all he had left was his paint and his brushes.

**

His daily outings became rarer and were eventually limited to the corner store. From time to time he would even ask the cleaning lady to bring some necessities when she came, so he didn't have to leave his apartment and go downstairs. However, once night fell, he always made his way out of the house to get to the exact same spot: his bridge. He sometimes spent the night there only to be awakened at the break of the following dawn by the sound of the truck come around to collect trash, the metallic rumbling was enough to pull him out of his lethargy.

He created paintings, filling canvas after canvas lit only by his floor lamp. But he was never satisfied with his

71

work. Each location represented in his work was some corner of Venice. This city where the light flickered into the smallest cracks, where the clarity of the sky was rivaled only by the sparkling green water of the lagoon, on Dave's canvasses everything became obscure. The bit of red that was visible among the grey and the black shone a shade closer to vermilion. It was all nothing more than the reflection of his sufferance, the feeling of eternally falling.

**

The wind whistled throughout the labyrinth of alleyways, whipping streams of rain against the facades of the homes lining the streets; winter was announcing its imminent arrival. Dave adjusted the scarf hanging around his neck, his hat was dripping. He arrived at the bridge of reflection when he noticed a man leaning over the parapet.

A thought suddenly came to him, there was possibly another who knew of this bridge's secrets. A mixture of anxiety and rage overtook him. And what if he altered the bridge? Then Lisa would be lost to him forever. He approached the man and asked what exactly he was doing.

"I'm working on the upkeep of all the city's monuments. Even under the rain! There was a loose stone so it's my job to evaluate the damage done, which is exactly what I'm doing now. Then, I make a report for an expert who decides what to do. We're tracking vandalism, but sometimes they come out to investigate old rocks, you see."

Everything happened so quickly, much more quickly than he could have imagined. He saw himself pushing this man over the side. As though in a silent film, the man hit his head against the edge of the canal before his lifeless body broke the water's surface. There was no noise made to be heard over the sound of the whipping winds and pelting of raindrops. All that remained was a sensation of moisture on Dave's hands. He disappeared around the corner of one of the many cold alleys of the city.

**

The next morning, it was under the continuing rain that the Commissioner Conti arrived at the police station at 7:30. He had taken a call from Lieutenant Zanioli an hour beforehand, informing him that a body had been discovered on the docks in Giardini by some local fishermen. Zanioli, a Venetian man from the neighborhood of Murano, had been the teammate and right-hand man of the Commissioner for two years and was awaiting a promotion to command the station in Padova where he lived with his wife and three children.

The police boat awaited the Commissioner, motor running, and his teammate, already boarded, held his hand out so as to help the Commissioner on. His foot had hardly touched the inside of the boat before the vessel was steering away from the dock.

"Information about the victim?" demanded the Chief.

"Not yet. The fishermen alerted us regarding the presence of a body stuck between the jacks at the terminal in Giardini. The forensics experts are already on the scene. We'll have more information once we arrive."

Sitting at the back of the cabin, the Commissioner looked out of the window. The rain and the wind were stronger than before, winter had certainly begun in Venice.

The boat crossed the canal at a quick, steady pace before turning left toward the docks. Arriving in Giardini, the star of the police force ordered the boat's captain to slow down so as to better approach the pier.

The forensic technician was waiting for instructions from the Commissioner.

"Hello Silvio."

"Hello Umberto. We've gone ahead and taken the first samples. We waited for you to begin removing the body."

The Commissioner made a gesture at the officers equipped with rope and the two agents began to approach the body. After securing the corpse with the ropes, they lifted it onto the riverbank. The ambulance boat had already brought two paramedics to the scene who were waiting under the cover of the quay for their orders to transport the corpse to the hospital for autopsy.

"Put it there, that way we'll stay dry at least. What terrible weather to die in!"

The doctor began taking different samples from the body.

"The suspense is too much under all this rain Doctor! Shed some light on the situation for us, let's get this over with!"

"Blunt force and drowning, the classic. But I'll need to confirm with an autopsy which one was the cause of death. Cranial Hematoma, blunt force trauma or a long drop. I imagine I'll find some contusions on the areas which came in contact with the ground, I'll share my report with you all. There are two options: he lost consciousness from the head injury and drowned, or the hit to the head was fatal. The second is more likely considering the position of the wound. I'll be able to confirm that by the end of the morning. As for the time of the incident, I would say between ten p.m. and midnight."

"Thank you, keep me updated about the results."

The Commissioner made another gesture at the paramedics who took the body away.

**

The return trip to the Commissioner's office took place in complete silence, and it was only after the heat of the coffee began to diffuse into his veins that the Chief began to speak again.

"Terrible weather. Terrible case! It's just one of those mornings…"

They all scattered about into their respective offices without another word.

An hour later, the Chief called Lieutenant Zanioli.

"Can you come meet me in my office?"

"I'll be upstairs in just a moment Commissioner."

**

The lieutenant knocked on the door only to signal his arrival before entering the Commissioner's office.

"I sent out photos of the victim to the department of research."

"Perfect, Lieutenant. On my end, I had an interview over the phone with the specialist of management of the lagoon and the canalways. Considering the currents and the tide from last night, they've concluded that the man was in the Castello area. I've got four different canals which come to a head in the dock area where the man was found. We need to review all of the surveillance videos. While we're waiting for a more exact time of death from forensics, we can start thinking about a time frame from ten last night to midnight. I sent the request and as soon as possible you'll go pick up the recordings. That should be around this afternoon, they told me. We're looking for an attack or an interaction between at least two individuals on a bridge or an embankment. Or a balcony. If there was any conflict, let's not exclude balconies as a possibility."

"A domestic dispute which ended badly?"

"I wouldn't want to pick a fight with his wife if that is the case!"

**

Back at his apartment, Dave immediately went to bed, dripping from the rain, frozen from the winds, and haunted by the scene which just played out before his eyes. It was, however, certainly him, he was the aggressor in that heinous act. He trembled from the cold, from the fever, and he mumbled himself into a feverish slumber.

"No, can't know...my secret...my Lisa. She's coming back."

**

The rain struck the shutters of Dave's bedroom window. It was already 9 in the morning when Dave emerged from his night filled with delirious hallucinations and nightmares. He woke up to the sensation that Lisa was there, by his side. The bitter reality struck him seconds later. There was only one thing left to do. He had to paint her to make her appear.

He stood up abruptly, slipped on his raincoat, grabbed his pencil case and left the apartment. Lisa's face was engraved in his mind, all he had to do was close his eyes to see her smile. He just had to go and see the spot again in order to perfectly recreate the background. He left in the direction of Giardini. He could use the flowers, or perhaps the trees and bushes, or maybe even capture the sky between rainstorms. As he approached Giardini, he noticed a troop of people surrounding the quay. Strangely, it was neither the time nor the place for tourists. He continued to approach his destination when he saw a police boat arrive and dock, then a group of officers exited the boat and disappeared into the crowd. Dave stopped and thought before choosing an adjacent alleyway which would allow him to continue without being seen.

The scene unfolding before him was not what he had imagined; the body of a man had been fished out of the water. Suddenly, the previous night came back to him. The stone, the bridge, his act, him fleeing.

He turned around and headed in the other direction.

Lisa's face would be good enough on its own.

**

Around three that afternoon, the lieutenant who went to the surveillance center came back to the Commissioner's office with the recordings from the neighborhood's cameras. He went directly to the Commissioner.

"Here, the USB drive with all of the videos requested, you can review them directly on your computer, the software is already installed."

"Thank you. If you don't mind, can you get it set up for us? I'm not very *good* with technology."

"No problem."

"While you're working on that, I'll get some coffee for us, it's the least I can do."

The lieutenant smiled as he sat down and plugged the thumb drive into the computer. It was always the same routine when it came to using modern tools. The Commissioner could have almost certainly done it alone, but he seemed to flinch in the face of technologies though he was always the first to applaud their effectiveness and the time they saved everyone. Maybe he did it because it was easier, maybe out of fear that he wouldn't be able to master the tool, in either case he preferred to delegate the task to another. The coffee prepared in the machine in his office was the best in the station, and they would be needing a fair amount considering the number of files copied onto the USB drive. He opened the software and began downloading the first series of videos. In the time it took to load this first section, the Commissioner had already placed two steaming mugs on the desk.

They began watching the videos at a more accelerated rate. The streets weren't crowded at that time, so the two risked nothing by scanning through the images at double speed. There was nothing at all in the first video, aside from a passerby and another person who crossed paths. A second video, then a third, a coffee refill, and still nothing. The images flashing before them were often blurred by the wind and the rain, occasionally there were stipples that formed, because of the movement of the lens and the raindrops which covered it, transforming the passing people into indistinct shapes for a few seconds. After the fifth video they still hadn't found anything of value to their investigation.

"Stop! There!"

The screen showed the bridge of reflection. A silhouette, from behind, was bent over the parapet of the bridge. Another person approached him, stopping mid-step.

"Okay, continue but slow it down."

"Okay. It looks like two men, considering their height and approximative weight. The man who's approaching is about 1m80 in height."

On the screen, the man was holding something rectangular in his hand. He stopped next to the other man who was leaning over the side.

"What's he doing, bent over like that?"

"Either he's crazy, or he's looking for something. In either case, he's really tempting fate."

The image went blurry. When the picture came back, the man had grabbed the other who was leaned over and taken him by the shoulders. The image scrambled again, just a few seconds, but long enough for the man to disappear from the screen. The other man, still standing a little to the right, had already taken off, galloping away.

"It's them!" Exclaimed the Commissioner. "It's the bridge of reflection. Let's go Lieutenant, we'll warn the forensics team on the way so, they can meet us there. Let's get a move on before the rain washes everything away!"

**

The boat worked its way up the canal, and then came to the foot of the bridge from the video. The Commissioner and the Lieutenant dismounted the boat and began investigating the area around the bank below the bridge.

Nothing. Not a single trace of blood. Rain washes away all traces of man.

"Commissioner, there's nothing here."

"Block off the area anyway, forensics will be here soon. I'm going up on the bridge to see if there's anything."

Commissioner Conti climbed the few steps that led to the bridge and leaned over the side like the man in the video had done before dying the night before. There was nothing interesting enough in the water of the canal or on the riverbank to captivate the attention of someone for that long a period of time. His gaze was held on the partition bridge, which seemed completely average. There were, however, scratches on the cement between two stones. Maybe the man scratched it himself, go figure what goes on inside of peoples' heads sometimes. He would have to ask the medics if they found deposits under the man's fingernails.

During this moment of reflection, the crime scene specialists arrived. A man and a woman dressed in all white jumpsuits approached, they nodded to the Commissioner and then began their work.

Commissioner Conti's cell phone rang.

"I hope you have good news for me, Doctor." began the Chief.

"I do actually, Umberto. In case you didn't know already, we have the identity of the man we found."

"Oh good! It's crazy when you think about it, we have an over equipped judicial service, armed to the teeth like Interpol, who are *supposed* to be able to give me results within the hour and it's *you* who ends up doing all the work in their place…? This is progress, I suppose."

"It's a combination of coincidences Commissioner. The medic who brought him in to the operation and examination room recognized him. His name is Giovanni Scalla. He's a relative of his, a distant cousin, but he lives in Venice too. He works for the maintenance and conservation department for public monuments in the area. That's about all that Marco, the medic, knows about him, they didn't see each other often."

"Thanks Silvio, I'm taking note of it. And the autopsy results?"

"Time of death, between 10:15 and 11:00 at night. I can't be any more precise than that, between the rain and the saltwater ...The trauma to the head was the cause of death. It corresponds with a fall from a height of about three meters onto stone, there were a few pieces of granite in the wound. We also found some silica under his fingernails. We find it most often in stones or in mixtures made to serve as mortar."

"I was just going to ask about that!"

"At your service! That's it for the main part, for the rest of the details, you can find it all in my report, I'll send it your way immediately."

"Thanks Doctor. See you soon."

"The later, the better!"

"You certainly said it."

The agents had begun blocking off the area with fluorescent tape. While one was taking photos of the impact zone, the other was taking samples of everything that could have been linked to the crime, whether directly or indirectly. The Commissioner went to join the Lieutenant.

"I just spoke to the examiner who confirms the cause of death was blunt force trauma. We have new elements now. The victim's name was Giovanni Scalla. He was fiddling around with the stones on the bridge, that's why he didn't get up when the other man approached him. We have to go back to the station and look at those videos again, this time we'll expand the perimeters. There has to be a camera that got his face on film when he was making his getaway.

**

The Lieutenant and the Commissioner stared at the screen for hours. It was already night, and the two still hadn't found anything of interest.

"We're going in circles Commissioner."

"Thanks, in case I hadn't already noticed. To think that I'm usually quite fond of our evenings spent one on one…"

"Who do you think you're talking to?"

"I would prefer to spend my night doing something else aside from treading water with this case. We have too little information, we're missing something."

A smile flickered across the Lieutenant's face.

"And I would be much better off at home taking care of my kids. I leave early in the morning and by the time I get back they're already in the bed. And they're growing so quickly, I feel like I'm missing everything."

"Yes, I understand, and you'll get your transfer! As for us, we'll get this guy. Let's restart from the beginning, go back to the video of the bridge, we missed something I'm sure."

The Lieutenant carried out the order.

"There, go back a bit more...STOP! Zoom in on what he's got in his hand."

The enhanced image was too pixelated.

"What do you see?"

"I would say a pouch, like for painting tools. We find them all over the place at the end of an artist's arm, they're all over town. It's not a solid color, I can see a drawing on it. There, it seems like eyes. Over here might be a mouth."

"Yeah, and there's a nose. It's a portrait, and if I can trust these little crumbs of electronic squares, that's some long hair, so it's likely a woman. Can we print it out cleanly?"

"If I fiddle with it a bit and send it to the superintendent's printer, I should be able to get something that's not too bad, I can't make any promises though."

"Perfect, I'll call him to let him know I'm coming to pick up these photos."

It was absolutely a painter's pouch, but this one had been personalised by its owner with a portrait of a woman. The black and white photo was precise enough for the Commissioner to discern the face of a beautiful woman. He couldn't actually know if the face belonged to a real person or if it was a creation of the artist himself, but he had singled out this pouch and its owner among the masses of artists whose shadows inhabited the City of Doges. This case would be laborious.

IV

It was hot in Rome at the start of this particular weekend in April, Lisa left her office and took a taxi to the train station. She had taken her suitcase with her that morning so she wouldn't have to double back to the hotel after work, meaning she could go straight to the station and take the train toward Milano. After five days being separated, she was happy to steal a few minutes from George and arrive before dinnertime.

Sitting in her chair in first class, she thumbed through the notes she had taken that week. These last few days had been fruitful for her and her team. They were able to find tombs from the 14th century more than eight meters below the surface, as well as some sepulchers. About a dozen of what was found were exhumed for the moment, but they were hopeful to extract others as well. Carbon 14 analysis allowed them to roughly estimate the date of the creation and usage of these tombs. But the element used to determine a clearer time frame, and what had fascinated Lisa, were the Hebraic inscriptions found on the stones. They retraced a part of history. It seemed as though they discovered an ancient medieval cemetery created by and for the Jewish community that was later abandoned, and the space was turned into a ghetto before being razed to the ground to make space for the city of popes in the 17th century. For a moment she thought back to Venice, and Dave, about how she had discovered some inscriptions a bit similar to these on the side of a bridge. In spite of the fact that her horrible relationship with Dave was less than a memory now, a chill ran across her arm despite the sun which shone bright across the window. She pulled her jacket on tighter. Maybe the air-conditioning was just up too high. She put away her notes and took out a book to occupy her mind until her arrival in Milano.

**

George had reserved a table at the Trattoria Toscana. It was only a few blocks away from their house and it was at this charming little restaurant that the pair had shared their first meal together. They had come back regularly, but for this evening George had something special planned to embellish the dessert course. He had taken a little detour to the jeweler's shop to pick up the ring, a solitaire-set diamond, that he chose for Lisa. Everything was prepared for his proposal.

**

The air was fresh this morning and the sun's rays were still a bit shy. The Commissioner marched in-step to the police station. He was ahead of schedule this morning and decided to stop, have a coffee and a croissant just before arriving at the Rialto bridge. He was seated on the terrace to be able to observe the awakening of the city.

He noticed Lieutenant Zanioli walking in a hurry toward the police station and he called out to him.

"Hey, Zanioli! You seem like you're in a rush this morning, come have a coffee with me!"

"Hi Commissioner! The train from Padova was on time but the motorboat was full, as per usual, so I preferred to just walk the rest of the way. I was hoping to get in early because I have new information regarding the Giardini case. But, since you're here, I can't turn down a little break."

"What'll you have?"

"A coffee, that should do."

He made a gesture in the direction of the server who left after taking the order while the Lieutenant took out his documents.

"So, the news is regarding the case?"

"Yes, I've got something to put some wind in our sails I think."

"That's unexpected!"

"Here's what I've got. Scalla was officially a service technician for the community, as you already know, but in the office in Rome, he shows up as a member of an 'Order', it's a pretty mysterious title I have to admit, linked to historical monuments. Some people presume that this Order has ties to a network of art trafficking, but it's only suspicions as nothing has actually been found."

"Hmm. That can explain it, maybe there was a settling of scores on that bridge. An exchange of some sort that went badly."

"Possibly. But, really all of this is just too blurry because nothing has been officially tied to this "Order", in terms of criminal activity."

"Do you have any more information on the matter?"

"I do, actually. I did a little digging and I came up with this."

He passed a paper to the Commissioner who read it.

"...a secret order composed of collaborators, the hierarchy of which is very complex. The preeminent members are mostly historians, but overall it's a network that's kept up by the concealment of information which is what allows them to remain so active."

"Okay, so it's another one of these many tentacled-networks, but they seem relatively inoffensive. But, keep reading, a little further down."

"... They're looking to prove the veracity of certain legends, myths, and other folkloric history linked to cities in order to rediscover lost treasures."

"Voilà. Basically, it's not a criminal organization, technically, and the member's files that are listed and available aren't representative of the totality of their membership, I'm sure of it. But those that we have reviewed, are clean. They're regular people with regular jobs. What must make this network so effective is the diversity of the...recruitment, I suppose. They've got eyes and ears everywhere and they pay for information we can assume, small amounts, but that vary according to the value of the information offered in exchange."

"I see. And Scalla was a part of this Order?"

"Apparently so. It seems he was, even though it's still somewhat unclear, but a low-ranking member. The type who received information from someone else, who got it from someone else and then he would act on it."

"Hmm. So, the hypothetical about an exchange gone badly is still plausible."

"Yes."

"And further, that interaction would have to be something connected to drawing or painting, given the pouch we saw in the surveillance video. But that's still too slim to confirm anything, of course."

"Exactly."

The Commissioner sighed.

"Okay, well let's keep our eyes and ears open too, then. In the meantime, I think it's time to get back to the station!"

**

A new case was handed to the Commissioner. There was a new network of distribution of counterfeit objects established in Venice and the entire region. It was an order issued from his superior, the superintendent. The mayor and the regional advisors had insisted that the Commissioner work the case as urgently as possible so that the distribution might be stopped rapidly. The illicit market was weakening the economy and began to affect the notoriety of the elected officials.

The Commissioner already had so much to manage and the cases that were sending him around in circles had to be put off to the side for the time he needed to solve this new one. The case of the murder on the bridge in Castello ended up buried at the bottom of a pile of ongoing investigations.

**

There were several holidays during the month of May, meaning that Lisa could take a mini vacation. The round trips between Rome and Milano were finished, at least for the week. George wasn't so lucky; he wasn't able to take that time off. That Thursday was a holiday, and he had a meeting scheduled for the following Friday in Venice. In his head, he intended to take advantage of the chance to take Lisa there to spend the weekend together.

They strolled through a park together not far from their home, enjoying the springtime sunshine on a Sunday afternoon.

"It's such a beautiful morning to be out walking!" She exclaimed.

"Yeah, the weather is splendid. It's a wonderful weekend."

"I think I'll come back alone on Monday since you'll be working. The calm, with the different birds' songs, it's so relaxing."

"You can come back every day if you want, but Thursday's a holiday and I have an appointment Friday morning in Venice. I was thinking maybe you'd come along with me and we could stay there the whole weekend."

Lisa stopped for a moment. She thought back to her stay in Venice with Dave. She was destabilized and didn't know how to respond to George who was waiting, overjoyed about what he felt was a romantic proposition. She offered an evasive response to hide behind.

"Why not? I just have to verify that I don't have anything scheduled for Friday."

"I thought it might be nice to go back there together."

"Yeah, of course, it's just that...I don't know, it's a little sudden, I wasn't expecting it. We'll see, okay?"

"Okay, come on let's go get a coffee over there."

The two of them walked toward the center of the park where there was a small café with a terrace. George didn't make any comments. He knew very well that a medical appointment, a show or an outing with her girlfriends at the last minute would have been just a pretext to get out of going.

The morning ended. Continuing their walk, they returned to their apartment. During their coffee break, Lisa thought about the incoherent response she had given to George. It was so stupid. Her relationship with Dave, that was in the past. She couldn't refuse to go to Venice with George just because of that. She spun the ring George had given to her around her finger, mindlessly. The weekend in Venice, George must have been thinking about it for a moment, he must want to spend the weekend relaxing together, and she had responded to the idea as if he proposed a weekend trip to a gulag. She was angry with herself. A weekend of relaxation could be really good for the two of them. Venice was big, it would have been virtually impossible for her to bump into Dave, and maybe he had even left town already. Also, all she would have to do is avoid the Castello neighborhood where Dave lived. Lisa stopped walking, she took George by the waist, moved in and kissed him. Then, she told him that she accepted his invitation, and that she couldn't wait to pretend they were Romeo and Juliet with him on the balcony of their hotel.

"But that was in Verona!"

"Who cares, as long as we're in love!"

George smiled at her, and without hesitating, in spite of his surprise, her grabbed her by the shoulders, pulled her to him and kissed her, tenderly.

**

Lord Ravagnelli left his house, the San Polo neighborhood, for his morning walk. He enjoyed walking the streets of Venice in the morning. This little stroll helped him stay in shape as he spent most of his time locked up in his office. And, in any case, he loved the feel of the city, its smells, its colors, its vibrations.

The commissioner of the Venice Biennial found a calm and an endless source of inspiration in the morning, as well as a breeding ground for artists which was incessantly renewing itself. As he did every day, he changed his path in the hopes of coming across some of the numerous artists, painters, sculptors, and musicians who were getting set up for a day full of creation in the serpentine back streets and alleyways. Artists for a single season, some disappearing in the direction of other cities once they had a bit of cash to line their pockets. There were also the sedentary ones, renting a room across town on the other side of the lagoon where it was more affordable, who made the daily trek into town to whet their undying thirst at the well of inspiration that is the City of Doges.

The sedentary ones, he knew quite well. He was looking for new members among their ranks. Was this a distraction, a simple walk or a real need to keep his sleuthing skills fine-tuned? It was of little importance. His wife, like so many others, told him he was simply wasting his time and that his reputation was sufficient for artists to gravitate toward him to present themselves and their work. However, he continued and felt proud that he was still able to dig up some real unexpected gems around a little unsuspecting street corner or back alley.

He crossed the Rialto bridge long before the shopkeepers opened their boutiques. He followed the street

Via San Lio, situated in front of the bridge just after the Campo de San Bartolomeo, heading in the direction of the Arsenal. He planned to branch out near Giardini to head back to his office.

His walking pace was rather rapid, the trademark of Venetians who walked onto and off of bridges with intent and agility as though it were nothing more than a sidewalk.

While leaving the plaza of Santa Maria Formosa, he noticed a painter before his easel, a binder in hand. He approached the man, sure to have never seen him here before. The regulars usually set up in the corners or just in the center of the plaza.

"Hello, I'm an amateur art collector and I am quite interested in new work and the artists that produce them. I have never seen you around here. Are you new to Venice?"

He always started his introduction in this way: make the painter feel as though he can trust him, make him understand that he wasn't just some onlooker come to disturb him while the painter is at work, and to dissolve the idea that he might be a work inspector or a tax auditor.

"Hello," responded the painter without raising his gaze from the canvas. "I don't usually come to places as big as this one. I don't do paintings for tourists, even if everyone needs some form of art, but I'm lucky enough to be able to exclude all of that which doesn't inspire me."

The tone of his voice was slightly haughty, although it didn't seem as though he wanted to end the conversation there. It was as though he was proud to be free and he was making an ostentatious show of that liberty. He seemed to want to take advantage of the moment to manifest this sense of pride in the face of the commissioner of the exposition.

"I can see that. Your representation of the cathedral is unlike all the others we find in the hands of tourists."

"I like to transcribe what I feel into my art; the messages from the monuments that I feel in the deepest part of my soul."

Ravagnelli allowed a silence to settle in between the two of them. He knew he would have to deal with this original artist who believed a bit too much in the character he had created, but who also had that little something that made all the difference in an exposition. This cathedral wasn't anything spectacular or magnificent, but in the hands of this painter it seemed like a condemned prisoner on its way to execution. A chill ran over him.

He broke the silence to ask if the painter had been in Venice for long.

"Yes, it's been about eight months. I'm American, but I came here from Paris. Initially I came for a few days, then a few weeks, then a few months. The magic of Venice, right?"

"Do you have other finished canvases or pieces awaiting their finishing touches?"

"I have a few at my home, mostly sketches. But it all still needs more work. There is so much to do to be able to express it all, they're so demanding."

"Carlo Ravagnelli. I'm Venetian and delighted to meet you Mr…"

"Dave Burnside."

"I would love to have a look at the rest of your work, if you will allow me."

Dave, still painting, nodded in the direction of his pouch where Ravagnelli found three canvases. He looked them over, attentively.

"Your paintings speak for themselves. You're far too critical when you say that they still need finishing. I think they're absolutely perfect, perfectly executed. I know artists are never satisfied, but I'm speaking to you from experience. These are wonderful pieces."

"Thank you. But I'm still dissatisfied the second I finish one, but once I start another one, I feel it's missing something that was present in the previous canvas."

"I see, I see. Listen, if you're interested, I would like to make a proposition: we can schedule a rendezvous so that you can show me all of your more "finished" work. I can come to your studio and make an inventory of all the pieces we can present."

"Present. What do you mean by that?"

Dave's paintbrush finally stopped.

"Oh, yes. I didn't finish introducing myself, excuse me. I'm the commissioner of the art exposition and I work for the Biennial of Venice. I can, and I would like to find a place for your work there. Next month, coincidentally, I'll be refreshing the artwork in five different wings, I would like to offer one of those spaces to you. You have a very specific vision of Venice. Your paintings should be seen by the outside world. It's important."

"I'll think it over."

"It's already thought over. Here's my card. Call me to confirm a time as well as the address of your studio. We'll put our heads together to figure out how to organize all the details."

That evening, on the first ring, Ravagnelli knew that it was Burnside calling, and that he was going to accept the meeting.

**

At 10:30 that morning, Ravagnelli left his office to go to the rendezvous in the Castello neighborhood. He found the front gate of the Venetian home immediately as indicated by Dave's instruction. He rang the third and final buzzer on the intercom as directed, and as warned it didn't bear the name Burnside.

"I'll open it up for you, it's on the second floor."

Ravagnelli pushed open the heavy door. When he arrived on Dave's floor, Dave was standing on the landing, he was wearing anthracite-grey linen pants, a white button-down and grey loafers.

"I see you've abandoned your painting outfit today, Dave. Is it alright if I call you Dave?"

"Of course."

"And you can call me Carlo."

"Alright then, Carlo. To be entirely honest, I finished my latest piece at nearly daybreak, so I haven't gotten much sleep. I just put this outfit on to make myself seem fresher and put together!"

"You wear it well! Oh, the life of an artist!"

He had hardly crossed the threshold and Dave was already presenting a canvas to Ravagnelli.

"My very last one. It's still fresh, I haven't varnished it quite yet... Where are my manners? Would you like a coffee?"

"No, thank you, I already had one at the office before coming here."

"I'm going to make one for myself, would you like another?"

"In that case, yes, I'll have one with you."

While Dave prepared the coffee, Ravagnelli took another look at the painting. This one was just as surprising as the one he had seen the day before depicting the cathedral, and it was just as satisfying. He looked around but didn't see another painting in the room.

"How many creations have you painted of Venice?"

"I would say about twenty as well as some charcoals, so nearly thirty altogether."

He came back from the kitchen with the coffee served on a platter.

"Coffee is truly man's best friend. Always faithful. It's one of the most therapeutic things in the world."

"I couldn't agree more! I would go so far as to say that it should be reimbursed by insurance like they do with other medications. Speaking, of course, about Italian coffee!"

"Oh well, that goes without saying. If I were president, I'd make you secretary of health, without a doubt!"

Dave raised his cup as though he were giving a toast, took a gulp though the drink was still burning hot, smiled with satisfaction and then moved toward a large wooden wardrobe with a lock on the front.

97

"They're all here. I lock them away for a multitude of reasons. The light, of course, but also dust and insects. But I'm also wary that a misguided individual might mistake them for paintings with a greater value and try to steal them."

You're right to be wary, we never know. Venice is a calm city, but there are some people who wouldn't hesitate to commit regrettable crimes for a few little objects to resell."

Dave took out his canvases one by one and leaned them against a china cabinet and any other available furniture surface.

Ravagnelli approached at his own pace, examining each piece with a close eye. Each piece represented a different corner of the city, but they all echoed the same emotion: the distress brought on by a great sufferance. The largest one, posed at the center of the china cabinet, depicted the basilica, the Duke's palace, and the bell tower with the lagoon in the distance. But on the ground, we didn't find the shadows of the two massive towers of granite, but rather the immense and gloomy one cast by a cruise ship covering entirely the walls and the ground of the little plaza. On yet another canvas, a canal with a bridge of stone overhanging, majestic and surrounded by the face of the palace and the villas. But on the walls, in the place of brick were the bloody stains which showed the violence of the water inflicted upon the edifices. The seemingly inoffensive ripples in the water engendered by the excessive passage of boats, the gondolas carrying millions of tourists, and the rising of the waters, which was only worsening in stride with climatic changes; all this water tirelessly lapped at the walls like so many imperceptibly fine blades shearing away the stone. Life. His life. His suffering exposed and naked before Ravagnelli's eyes, his throat was tight and dry. This was powerful. This was real. This was why he loved his career.

"I'm not sure it's such a good idea to consecrate a whole section just for my work. I don't think it will translate well before a large audience. You haven't said anything, are you disappointed? I don't paint with the idea of exposing my work in a gallery, maybe I need more time to refine all of this so it will be more...I don't even know... presentable?"

"Not at all, far from it, I'm just speechless, I'm contemplating that's all. It's so powerful, what you're able to transmit through your art. It takes time to take it all in."

"If even you aren't ready, that's a sign that the rest of the world isn't either. I don't feel prepared to talk to people about my work, respond to people and all of that."

"I think I have enough experience to assure you that nobody is ever truly prepared for that. But I can guarantee you that the public needs to see you, and your work. I will help you, for communication and publicity, that's my role. And as for the more pressing details; you won't need to pay for anything, I'll handle all the fees. You just need to show up and be there at the opening, have a drink with art collectors and amateurs of the art scene, lovers of your art, and believe me there will be plenty."

**

It was 12:30 when Ravagnelli left Dave's home. Even though there were still a few details to work out with Dave with regards to the showcase, he planned to tie up all the remaining loose ends over the phone. He set off in the direction of his home where he would be having lunch with his wife. Antonella was a talented chef. She prepared sumptuous dishes which her husband tried as often as possible. It was nothing like the salad bar where he normally ate to avoid having to prepare food for himself while Antonella was in class for the day. She was a professor at the University of Venice in the language department.

They lived at the top of a two-floor building with no elevator, like most of the apartment buildings in Venice. Once he entered the hallway, the familiar smell of a good risotto came and danced around his nostrils. He climbed the stairs, encouraged all along the way by the promise of a good meal as reward for the effort.

Once he entered the apartment, he exclaimed:

"Ah! That smell alone is enough to get the taste buds working in overdrive!"

"You're quite the little gourmand, I hope you know that," Antonella responded.

"It's ready, I don't have much time, so we can start eating now if you would like and you can tell me all about your new finds while we eat."

"Yes, yes of course."

They were seated at the table, there was a salad to go with the risotto. Carlo served the two of them, all while beginning his story.

"So, it's a young painter, but a true artist, and he doesn't even know it yet. As per usual, he doesn't feel ready to show his work, but I can guarantee you that the canvasses I saw at his place today were worth the detour."

"Is he Venetian?" Asked Antonella.

"No, he's American, but he's doing a tour of Europe to paint. However, as soon as he arrived in Venice, he hung his hat for a bit longer than he had anticipated. I don't know very much about him, but his paintings speak so loudly. The streets, the monuments, the canals and homes of Venice serve as his running theme, but it's nothing like the paintings used just as decoration, the ones that look just like the postcards we find sold in kiosks. In his work, I see a wounded Venice, a city that cries out and curses the attacks it suffers. But, through it all, it's the artist who retells his life's story, who talks about his experiences. A love destroyed or abandoned. Sometimes, there's a wink of hope that it will return, sometimes an abandonment of all hope. He paints his emotions and sees only one city with which he can identify. When you see his work, you'll understand. He's going to be a sensation.

"Wow, well thank you Mr. Commissioner of Exposition! You've sold me completely on your project. It's rare to see you this enthusiastic! Have you two been able to decide on a date?"

"Yes! He finally agreed to participate in the showcase, and we decided on a date for next month."

While talking, they finished their meals, and afterward, Carlo returned to work.

**

That afternoon, the Chief was in his office. Filling out paperwork and investigative reports was far from being his favorite activity, but he had resolved to sacrifice a half-day from time to time in order to get it done. The telephone rang. A familiar voice saved him from the monotonous task at hand.

"Hello Mr. Chief Superintendent."

"Hello to you Mr. Chief of Exposition! Oh, Carlo! you know you don't call often but when you do, it's a real pleasure. And your timing is perfect, I was starting to get bored typing up all of these reports."

"Everyone knows that my calls are rare but always top quality, and for your information, I was chosen to be the managing director of the biennial!"

"Congratulations my friend!"

They had known each other since childhood. Separated at the start of university, then reconnected by life's good fortune as adults, they could certainly call each other friends without hesitation.

"I've got two invitations waiting for you for the new exhibit. The opening night is happening next Saturday. I unearthed a real diamond this time, albeit in the rough, but it's breathtaking nonetheless."

"Oh, you and your talents! But don't tell me anything more, I want it to be a surprise. I'll talk to Maria about it and I'll get back to you."

"Perfect! And we'll all eat together after a few drinks, of course."

"With pleasure. It's been such a long time, and our wives will be happy to finally see each other again."

**

When the Commissioner left the office to head home, it was already nearly 8 in the evening. The day had been long and tiring. The last few stairs left to climb before arriving at the door to his apartment seemed unending.

"Good evening," he offered this as a greeting to alert his wife to his return before heading in the direction of his recliner, taking two glasses and lowering himself into the chair.

"I have two glasses awaiting a nice cold white wine!" She said aloud so that her husband might hear her in the other room. "Can you grab the bottle from the refrigerator and join me for some well-deserved drinks?"

Her husband took the bottle and joined her in the living room.

"And what have you done to deserve this sweet nectar? Is Venice finally rid of all its armed thieves, and traffickers of all sorts?"

"No, and it's awfully utopist of you to hope so. But this wine will help me remember that there are still good things in the world in spite of it all. Other than you, of course!"

She poured two glasses. They clinked their glasses together, proclaiming:

"To hope!"

The commissioner sighed a sigh of relief after his first swallow.

"Carlo called me today at the office."

"Carlo Ravagnelli? Wow, it's been a long time since we've heard from them."

"Yes. He says he's dug up a new painter and they plan to organize a showcase of his work. We're invited next Saturday. It gives us an occasion to see them, what do you say?"

"I think that's a great idea! And it gives me a chance to wear my new dress somewhere. But I haven't been able to find a bracelet to go with it, I'm thinking of just wearing it with a pearl necklace."

"I had a feeling you might say that! A pearl bracelet that I find completely by chance this week, would that work for you?"

"I think if we force chance's hand a bit, yes that might work."

V

George and Lisa left their car in a private parking lot and headed toward the taxi boat. The driver helped them load and organize their baggage on the small boat.

Lisa went down to sit in the boat's cabin while George gave the driver the address.

"Where are you two lovers headed?" Asked the conductor before George could even give the address.

George was a bit shocked by the frankness of the man, but he responded:

"To La Giudecca hotel, it used to be the old factory. I hope there are no rats left!" He said, smiling.

"Oh, I see! Excellent choice sir. I would love to spend all my nights in hotels like that! Even if there were still a few rats scattering around in the kitchen! But, I'm certain you two won't see any. The community went to work and did everything they needed to get rid of those little rodents, and the entire island has been rid of them as well."

"Yes, I'm sure you're right, and even if there are a couple left that gives the cats something to do. They have to get their exercise one way or another!"

George joined Lisa in the cabin area and the boat rode the waves in the direction of their hotel.

When George went to Venice on business related matters, he stayed in hotels situated near San Marco Plaza so he could be nearer to his colleagues and move forward with his research project, which was coordinated all across Europe. For this weekend with Lisa, he preferred to spring for a room in a hotel on Giudecca island. This way, Lisa could relax in the hotel's spa and take advantage of the pool as well as local shops while George was in and out of his meetings.

The hotel was built on an old industrial site and had been renovated using the red brick walls from an out of service factory seen as an emblem of Italian architecture. Because it was separated the canal of San Marco plaza, the hotel offered a panoramic view of the city of Venice. George hadn't hesitated for even a moment before reserving the room for their romantic return to Venice together.

**

Leaning over the hotel room's window, Lisa rediscovered Venice from a far more favorable viewpoint. Her thoughts hadn't turned, not even momentarily, toward her first experience here in Venice, she was in such awe of the panorama before her eyes. George walked up behind her and wrapped himself around her tenderly.

"I met the most beautiful woman in the most beautiful city. I am a truly lucky man!"

She turned around, smiling and embraced him. He held her tighter in his arms and together, the two of them made the short journey to the bed.

**

It was already well into the evening when George and Lisa begrudgingly left their room to get something to eat, they were uncertain about finding a restaurant nearby that would be open so late.

They had barely been seated at their table when Lisa noticed one of the curators from the British Museum who was eating with a man, she hadn't been able to place. The countless hours she had spent in the British Museum while she wrote her thesis in London had led her to meet Jasper, he was incredibly helpful when she found herself before the extensive collections.

Their meal finished, Jasper approached their table and invited the couple to come to one of the lounges and share an unmissable Limoncello.

"Would you like to have a drink?" Said Jasper to George.

"That's very kind of you," responded George who turned toward Lisa and asked if she wasn't too tired.

Yes, she was tired and would happily go back up to the room with just George, but politeness obliged her to accept, she couldn't offend Jasper who seemed so giddy about the coincidence.

"With pleasure! But I'm afraid my stomach won't be able to handle another drink."

"Come on! Follow me." Said Jasper in his signature tenor.

He was a rather corpulent man in spite of his average height, but during conferences he didn't have any need for a microphone. Inside of his massive packaging, ornamented with an abundant beard, dwelled the soul of a soft and jovial man. Lisa had compared him many times to a bear, but with a marshmallow center.

"Your stomach will feel much better once you've tasted this exquisite Limoncello. Afterwards, you might even finish the evening in a nightclub."

"Whoa there! No, more than anything, I'll be knocking out on my pillow, assuming I can make it all the way upstairs to my room!"

After getting more comfortably seated in the lounge, Jasper introduced the person with whom he had dined.

"Horacio Tucci is my Venetian colleague. We met here in Venice to organize the international conference of Mediterranean museums and antiques. Tomorrow we're expecting our colleagues from France, Spain, and Greece."

"Pleasure to meet you!" Said Lisa and George in symphony.

"Horacio, this is Lisa Wood, an old, and very serious student that I had the pleasure of helping during her research for her thesis. She was under our care. I always admired her hard work and stubbornness. I offered her a position on our team, but she turned it down with her signature elegance!"

"Horacio, we've already talked about that! It's very kind of you," responded Lisa. "But I'm passionate about my position in Rome and I don't count on changing that anytime soon."

"Passion, you say. It seems like her stubbornness isn't working in your favor now Jasper!" Said Horacio. You're going to have to lure her in better than that if you want her to leave Rome for England's perpetual drizzle!"

"Ha! You're very right about that, my friend! So, let's drink to our passions!"

**

The next morning, when George opened his eyes, it was already 9 o'clock. He only had an hour left to get ready.

"Long night." he said to Lisa who was just opening an eye.

"You're telling me! I drank too much of that sweet, citrusy potion. It's a treat, but the fogginess the day after is all the denser!"

"Then maybe you should open your other eye, things should be a bit clearer that way." Said George, all the while limbering up his body from the short night's sleep.

She threw a pillow at him, it missed.

"I'm going downstairs to get a little bite to eat, get some more rest and I can bring you up a coffee and some croissants."

"I would like that. That way I can take a shower and clear my head a bit more. I'll come down later to make a reservation with the esthetician and a massage session for today. I'll be here during your meeting. Idleness and a little pampering! It's exactly what I need!"

After leaving the breakfast platter in Lisa's room, George left to take the motorboat. He went to Palazzo Barocci where the managers of the lagoon were waiting for him, gathered in the meeting space of the hotel. When he entered, the assembly room was already full. In addition to the managers he had already met, he made a mental note of the representative from UNESCO and a representative of the office of the Minister of the Environment. The morning was going to be long, he said to himself.

At this moment, Lisa was in the hotel's spa. Her program consisted of full body massage, facial, and a full manicure. George was meant to meet her back at the hotel for lunch at around one in the afternoon. Her phone rang while Silvia, the young esthetician was painting her toenails. It was George. They were taking a break, but the meeting was still going on, and they were getting food brought in so, he wouldn't be meeting her for lunch.

"Don't worry," she responded. "I've got a full schedule for the day. You'll probably find me laying out poolside. I hope they don't keep you until dinnertime," she said ironically, "if they do, my skin will be burnt to smithereens when you get back!"

George laughed and then ended the call. A message appeared on his screen almost instantaneously.

"Come back soon. I love you."

They had made a habit of ending their calls with a written message when they were around their colleagues. Her words didn't encourage George to go back into the stuffy assembly room. He thought about how he should have made up some excuse to get out of coming to the meeting that morning. These kinds of meetings were always sterile and relatively pointless, and in any case the only result of these meetings was to schedule another in the near future where the problem still wouldn't be resolved.

He sighed and headed back into the conference, dreaming of Lisa sitting poolside.

**

After an idle morning of relaxation and a good meal, George had proposed that Lisa do a bit of shopping. The deluxe shops were all grouped together in the San Marco neighborhood where they were staying, the others bordered the streets and alleys closer to the neighboring areas.

George was supposed to go and visit Dave after months without any word. A short while before, George had received a call from Dave who proclaimed that he had finally solved the riddle from the bridge. But the content of the call was very unclear. He spoke about a discovery he made concerning another stone from the bridge that gave the key to solve the enigma, about strange dreams inside of which he found himself without really understanding how, and he discussed all of this in an unintelligible and complicated haste which the low call quality made even more impossible to decode. George was worried about him. He didn't know if what he heard was born of a drunken spell which caused Dave to confuse reality and dreams, or if it was just a run-of-the-mill phase of deliriousness. He had successfully slipped in, between two speeding trains of verbal nonsense, that he would be stopping by to see Dave the next time he came to Venice to clear everything up.

George knew that Lisa had completely moved past her experience in Venice and he never brought up the subject in detail, so when he went on his work trips, he never shared too many details with Lisa about his time in the *Serenissima*. Lisa never really posed any questions either and he had come to respect this silence, and in doing so he had never talked to her about his painter friend and the relationship the two had built surrounding the mystery of the bridge.

The two of them took the boat from the hotel that was able to cross the Salute canal and get to Piazza San Marco. Once arrived at the dock, the pair crossed the plaza, and before they had properly arrived at the road where the shops were grouped, George suggested that Lisa get started on her shopping while he went to see an old friend for a quick visit. They decided to meet back in two hours near the

111

Rialto, the bar next to the statue of Goldoni. This was the halfway point for both of their paths and would allow Lisa to take a shopping break.

Lisa started on the street that branched away from the Piazza San Marco, in the shadow of the belltower, heading toward Rialto. She stopped before a display window where each dress was more beautiful than the last. While she was studying the display, the bellowing voice of a bear escaped from a nearby circus said to her:

"You should choose the blue one, it would look marvelous on you, Madame."

Lisa turned around and smiled at the oversized teddy bear that was Jasper.

"You're still in Venice? I thought you had already left."

"I'm leaving this evening, but not before buying some perfume for my wife. Otherwise, I might as well not go back!"

Lisa laughed heartily at the image of this lumbering man offering a little gift to his beloved, the thin and frail Margaret.

"I've been going in circles for hours! Not really, I'm just being dramatic. I just don't know what to choose, and since I keep going around smelling everything, all the scents are starting to resemble one another. So, I'm still empty-handed trying to get some air to recapture some sense of smell."

"You've started to help me choose a dress; I can help you with the perfume."

"Really? I don't want to take up too much of your time."

"I'll try on the dress and after we can go to the perfumery. I have the whole morning to do my shopping."

They entered the store and Lisa asked to try the dress in the window. The saleswoman brought out three different colors and spread them out before Lisa. A few moments later, Lisa emerged from the fitting room in the blue one.

"Splendid! It looks wonderful on you!" Exclaimed Jasper.

"Yes," said the saleswoman, "it's an excellent choice. It's a chiffon dress, so it's very light to wear and we also have a matching jacket to wear during the evenings."

"Bring it to her, please," Jasper responded spontaneously, "That way you'll have an outfit for all of the soirees to come. You'll have plenty of occasions to wear it in Milan, Venice, Rome or hopefully even London!"

Lisa responded, a bit uneasy, that she hadn't planned to buy an entire outfit, but Jasper cut her off:

"It will be my gift to you. I owe you at least that! You dealt with me during your thesis and now I'm involving you in my perfume purchases."

"Oh, Jasper, I'm a little embarrassed, but thank you. And I have to correct you, you're a dear friend and far from being unbearable! It was a delight to study with you."

"Okay, okay, enough with the gratitude. Let's get this outfit on you so we can see how it looks."

Lisa put on the jacket that the saleswoman had gone to retrieve and then turned to face the mirror.

"This outfit was made for you Lisa. George is going to find you absolutely ravishing."

Lisa thanked Jasper once more and the both of them headed to the perfume shop.

Once the perfume was chosen and wrapped as a gift, Lisa and Jasper parted ways, but not before Lisa promised to come and visit the couple on her next visit to England.

**

George headed off in the opposite direction. He passed in front of the red granite lions and turned behind the Basilica and down one of the alleyways which led to Dave's house.

When he arrived in front of the building, he rang the buzzer regardless of the fact that the door was wide open. He heard music resonating in the corridors and thought to himself that if the noise was emanating from Dave's apartment, the neighbors must be displeased, and vice versa. In either case, the music was loud enough to mask the sound of the buzzer, which resulted in George taking to the stairs in spite of a lack of response and he wanted to see if Dave was home. The loud music was coming from the floor below Dave's which made George smile to himself, Dave must be thrilled, especially if he was trying to concentrate on painting at that moment. Dave's door was open as well, and he poked his head inside but was met without a response, yet again. Dave must have stepped out to run an errand. George decided to step in and wait inside the apartment rather than the hallway.

Standing in the corner of the entryway, he scanned the room which had been transformed into an artist's studio. Dozens of canvases had been leaned against surfaces here and there, most of which were unfinished as far as he could tell. George felt overtaken by a sense of discomfort while examining them. The colors he was using were nothing like the light of the city, and instead they communicated a troubling feeling. Yes, that was exactly it, the paintings were dark, the colors were muddy, and it represented nothing about the Venice that he knew.

His gaze stopped suddenly upon a painting that was half hidden by one of the more somber ones. The colors were pastel. A beaming lighthouse amongst this sea of grey! George crossed the room and held the canvas. It depicted a bridge, on which a woman was standing, focused and facing the painter. George immediately recognized his Lisa. His chest tightened and his mind tried to analyze the meanings and consequences of his discovery. Lisa had certainly experienced some painful moments with Dave which pushed her to leave Venice spontaneously and never look back. He thought back to the few moments when Lisa had spoken about Dave. Had she ever mentioned his name? He didn't think so, but would he have made the connection? Had she only spoken about Dave's career? Nothing came to him clearly. Everything remained vague and blurry in his mind and began to intermingle with the conjectures he was formulating at that moment. Only one thing was apparent to him: Lisa was alone in Venice. He thought about the Dave's bizarre behavior over the phone and this dark and dismal landscape of painted canvas before him. He was worried. He can't meet Lisa. He threw the painting to the ground and rushed off to meet with Lisa.

**

Lisa arrived at the Goldoni statue, George had yet to arrive at the bar, but she decided to head over anyway, and she took a seat on the terrace. She had decided to wait for

115

him, but sitting down, her feet were exhausted! She ordered a glass of water while she waited.

**

Dave left his apartment to go to the showroom. Zanioli was waiting for him there to make the final checks before the opening that night, but he had hesitated for so long before actually leaving that he was now running incredibly late. He took a detour across the Cannaregio neighborhood to buy some tubes of paint that he needed, after all, Zanioli could wait a bit longer. And he couldn't have cared less about how or where his paintings were installed. Even the crowd that would be coming to violate his work with their gaze and their commentaries and critiques wrought with unfounded judgement, who were they? What did they want? To enter into his mind, steal his thoughts? To discover his secrets, his *secret*. Not that, they won't get that. They won't steal my bridge.

In step with his thoughts, his pace quickened and became harsher. He was heading straight for the exhibit where the opening would take place. He convinced himself that he needed to take back his paintings, remove them from the view of the masses. While walking, he began murmuring to himself a multitude of questions followed by their responses in a delirious monologue.

Suddenly, as if stopped by a wall, Dave stopped at the plaza where the Goldoni statue indicated the direction of the theater. Dave, with bewilderment in his eyes and his body nailed in place, stared fixedly in the direction of the Bartolomeo bar.

He was staring at a woman, seated on the terrace, a glass in her hand.

His Lisa. She was there.

She had come back. I knew that all those dreams were more than just mere illusions, that all of this, all that I've done, served a purpose. I'll be able to get her back, we'll be happy. Yes, we'll be so happy. It was really Lisa, she was there, on the terrace, with a drink in her hand.

Dave walked toward the bar. Lisa was looking around, not really focusing on anything in particular, waiting to spot George at any moment. As if in a nightmare, it was Dave who entered into her field of vision. He was walking towards her, entranced by her presence, and she was overcome with a feeling of panic. She wanted to uncross her legs and stand up, but nothing happened. Her body refused to move, the ice cubes in her glass repositioned themselves in her as they melted, the clinking sounds reverberated and caused her hands to tremble. He was right next to her now, she tried to convince herself that nothing bad was going to happen, there was nothing dramatic about crossing paths with an ex by chance. Dave was moving more quickly than she anticipated and she was even more surprised when he lurched at her and grabbed her by the wrist, pulling her toward him. She didn't want to get up, but the pain in her wrist forced her to follow the movement. She heard Dave's voice as though from a great distance, enveloped in a cloud of fog too dense for the reality of his words to penetrate. He told her to follow, to come with him, that she belonged to him and that everything would go back to how it was before, they would never leave one another's side again. She blurted something out that not even she understood, and she tried to resist. Her bracelet couldn't stand up to the sheer force of the interaction and it broke, spreading pearls all across the ground. She lowered her head and watched them roll in all different directions,

117

but Dave was already pulling her, this time much harder, and he dragged her down the underpass of San Lio in the direction of his apartment.

The two marched on in silence for several meters. Dave had slightly loosened his grip on Lisa's wrist, the surprise effect had dissipated, and she hoped to be able to have a more reasonable conversation with him. She stared at him out of the corner of her eye. He had changed considerably since she left him. His face was almost weather-beaten, he was poorly shaven, and all of his features aged him terribly, the neglect made it all the more drastic.

She started to gather herself, and the fogginess in her mind began to clear. He didn't seem like he could be reasoned with. He had taken up the same litany of phrases he had spilled out at the bar, this time adding in new ones, cutting himself off mid-sentence, speaking sometimes with a strong voice and at others barely more than a whisper. She uttered the start of a phrase and he cut her off swiftly, threatening her if she didn't remain calm and quiet, and tightening his iron grip around her wrist.

"You're never leaving me again, you're mine."

**

George arrived at San Bartolomeo square. Lisa wasn't sitting on the terrace. He felt a twinge of something, perhaps anxiety, when he looked at his watch, they had definitely decided on this time to meet. Maybe she had decided to wait for him inside the bar instead. He walked amongst the tables that were set up in the plaza. His foot crushed something hard which broke under his weight. He looked toward the ground and noticed pearls, mostly crushed and others were completely broken, as well as the chain that once linked them to one another. Without hesitation, he leaned over and picked them up, some of the pearls were still attached to the closure. He recognized Lisa's bracelet, a souvenir which he had gifted to her when he came back from a conference in Athens at the end of the previous year.

Chills ran across his skin. He understood immediately what must have happened before he arrived.

He had gotten there too late. They must have run into each other, and there was an argument that ensued. What an awful coincidence that they should cross each other's paths, with all of the streets and alleys of this city! It was like something from a bad movie, or at least just a movie which he would have hardly found amusing. Where were they? He couldn't give in to the panic. He tried to call Lisa's phone out of instinct, but as expected, she didn't pick up. Where could they have possibly gone? Did he take her back to his apartment? Of course, if not where else? He didn't see any other possibility.

He set off in the direction of Dave's building.

**

The Chief Commissioner and his wife were getting ready to go to the opening of the exposition. She was sitting at her vanity putting the finishing touches on her makeup when he held out a jewelry box to her, it was from Orlandonis', a jeweler situated on the Rialto bridge.

"Who should I thank, you or luck?" She said, rebelliously.

"Me, obviously."

119

She opened the shell case and saw a magnificent pearl bracelet.

She gave him a smile before kissing him very tenderly so as not to disturb her lipstick.

"It's absolutely wonderful! Thank you so much. I'm already Mr. Commissioner, we can leave now."

The entrance to the Biennial art exposition was guarded by a security agent who checked the invitations of all those who entered as well as the continents of all handbags. Once they had passed the security checkpoint, they followed the hall in the direction of the exposition pavilion. The decor was splendid, and the lighting was the perfect compliment. His friend Carlo had once again outdone himself; the exhibit would have given any other renowned art museum a run for its money. The walls had been upholstered with a material to represent the interior of a palace, the paintings hung from these walls while a reproduction of a Venetian bridge dwelled at the center of the showroom, acting as a platform for other paintings in the exhibit. The decor had been put in place, all that remained was for the curious hearted to discover the work of Burnside.

The paintings were breathtaking, and the Commissioner and his wife walked in silence through the gallery, completely submitted to the beauty and density of the pieces. Maria wandered away from the corridor toward the cardboard and wood bridge which resembled perfectly one of the bridges of stone one might find in Venice. She stopped in front of a canvas and looked for her husband. He had crossed the room and stopped before one of the only portraits in the exhibit. She tried to get his attention, but he was already totally absorbed by the image, so she went to join him.

"You completely changed the direction of the circuit?"

"No, it's just this portrait, it drew me in," he said. "I feel like I know this woman, it's strange."

"It must be the artist's muse. It's funny, he hasn't used the same palette here as he does in the others. It seems like he's nostalgic. It must play some part in recounting the story that Burnside is trying to tell us."

The Commissioner didn't respond immediately. His wife took his arm, ready to continue taking in the exhibit with him when he exclaimed:

"Yes! That's what it is, I *have* seen her already! It's the face of the woman that was painted on the artist's pouch that the man was carrying the night of the murder on the bridge. Shit! That's exactly what I needed tonight. Did you see the painter when we came in?"

"No, I don't think I saw him, but wait, you think this is the man you're looking for?"

"I have no idea, but I have to follow any leads I can get. Continue with the visit, I'm going to find Carlo."

Carlo was in the center of a group of Japanese spectators, in the middle of what seemed to be a rather mundane discussion. He approached a few steps at a time and nodded in a way so as to indicate that Carlo come over to him. Carlo excused himself from the group and went to join him.

121

"Thank you, you saved me, they wouldn't let me go! It seems like you weren't really there to save me, you seem too worried, what's wrong?"

"Nothing in particular, but I'd like to meet the artist, can you introduce me to him?"

"Of course, but you're not fooling me. You've got the look of a police chief, not of a friend who's come to enjoy himself for an evening with his wife."

"It's most likely nothing. But to sum it up, a few months ago a man was murdered, pushed off of a bridge by someone. The case has just been stagnating ever since, but among the clues we have, the man who did it had a large pouch with a portrait of a woman's face who looks a lot like that painting over there. If your painter is the owner of that pouch, obviously I have to know."

"I can understand, of course. But it's maybe not the best moment to...confirm that suspicion."

"Don't worry, I'm not going to start yelling 'police' and putting him in handcuffs. I'll be very discreet; I'll ask him a few questions and then ask him to come by the station tomorrow."

"Of course, of course. I haven't seen him yet; he still hasn't arrived. And now he's more than an hour late. He didn't really seem all that enchanted at the idea of an opening night, I hope he won't let me down. Let's go and check outside to make sure he's not lurking around out there, that sometimes happens; a bit of stage fright at the last minute."

The two men went outside, but they found nobody in the courtyard aside from the security guard who hadn't seen a man meeting their description.

"Do you have his address? I'm going to give him a little courtesy visit."

"Okay. Hang on, I'll put the address in your phone, it's pretty easy to find. It's the second floor, third button on the buzzer. Call me when you get to his building so that I know if I have to continue without him this evening and if… If you find out anything less pleasant."

Carlo went back inside of the pavilion and the Commissioner went in the direction of the town center.

**

Lisa was in a panic. Once again, she saw this staircase, she crossed the threshold she thought she had forgotten. Only the inside had changed. The furniture was littered with unfinished pieces. The ground was strewn with debris from cut up cardboard, crumpled paper, there were paint stains spread out and splattered underneath the easels. However, it wasn't the disorder that shocked Lisa most when she entered the apartment, but the dense air that hung over them, saturated with the smell of paint and a bitterness. The shutters, closed, only let in the slightest bit of light and in this disorder, she felt like she might suffocate.

Dave pushed her inside and closed the door behind them. He remained there, staring at her, his eyes glistening.

"You came back to me Lisa! We'll be so happy now that we're back together again. My wishes came true because of that bridge! Do you remember that bridge Lisa? It wasn't a dream! Are you thirsty? Do you want something to drink? You are so beautiful! You have to change, so you'll be gorgeous for the opening of my exhibit! I'm such a fool, of course you don't know, I'm exposing my art! That part wasn't a dream!"

123

The questions and responses spilled out one after another without waiting for her to respond. Lisa realized that Dave had lost his mind. He was no longer the painter that she had known in Paris. What could have possibly happened to him to make him this way? Why was he talking about dreams and wishes and the bridge? What bridge? Was it the same bridge where she had found the engraving? She had long since forgotten about all of that. At this moment, the only thing that mattered to her was that she was alone with him and she was scared. She finally interrupted him:

"Stop Dave! You're scaring me! What is happening to you? Do you see how you've been living? You know it's just a coincidence, that I just happened to be there by chance? I didn't leave you the way I did just to come back to you later on. I was very clear in my letter, you know me."

Dave shook his head 'no' frantically.

"I met someone. I live in Milan with him. I am happy now; you have to let me go. It's wonderful that you're exposing your work, you know…"

Dave interrupted her brusquely.

"NO! No and no! That's not how it works! It's not possible. It's the bridge, I know it is. You're going to come with me. Let's go. We're going to the bridge and you're going to recite the words and you're going to be with me forever, I know it!"

Lisa started to regain confidence and got more firm with her voice of protest.

"I am not going anywhere with you! You're out of your mind!"

She took advantage of the fact that the path to the door was clear and she rushed toward the exit, but Dave grabbed her by the waist and threw her on the couch.

"You need to relax Lisa! Do you not understand that? You're *mine*!"

He threw his hand forward and when it connected successfully with the side of Lisa's head, she lost consciousness.

**

George ran as fast as he could while weaving through the crowds of onlookers which peppered the city under the light of the lampposts. The crowds that normally overtook the streets and sidewalks of Venice had dissipated, but there were still enough large tourist groups gathered here and there at the base of a staircase, on a bridge, or a wall, all trying to immortalize each stone with their camera and hinder the George's progress.

Dave's apartment wasn't much farther. He crossed the little plaza, turned the corner and found himself before Dave's building. The door downstairs was still wide open. The thought crossed his mind that maybe Dave still hadn't come back home and all of this was just inside of George's own imagination, he was fully ready to accept this, to calm himself, to realize that all of this was just a terrible trick his mind had played on him and that Lisa wasn't with him, wasn't in danger and that she was just waiting for him somewhere else, and all of this was just a big misunderstanding. Just a misunderstanding. He decided to climb the stairs anyway, two at a time, unable to fully trust his own imagination, he arrived at the threshold of the door. He rang the bell.

**

The doorbell rang out. Dave was in the room, at Lisa's bedside, he had set her down on the bed after she lost consciousness. He closed the bedroom door and went to open the front door. Behind the half-open door was George, short of breath and trying to force a friendly smile.

"Hey, Dave! How are you? I'm here, back in Venice as we discussed! So, I thought I might pop by and we could grab a drink to catch up. It's been an eternity!"

"At least, yeah! But this evening I won't be available, I'm already running late, I've got to get to the opening of my exposition, I…"

"Oh yeah, you mentioned that, that's great!" George responded while taking a step forward.

"If you'd like, I can come inside for a minute and I'll come wi-"

"No, no not really. It's not a good time, come back tomorrow. I've got to finish getting ready and then take off."

Dave must have changed position because the door was ever closed just a bit more than at first and George had to contain himself to prevent him from placing his foot in the doorway. Something happened, he was sure of it, Dave didn't seem to be acting natural.

"Come on, I'll go with you, we always need a friend at moments like this. And I think I've earned the right to come and admire the paintings as well!"

"No, really I can't. I'm waiting for someone to come and pick me up, we're supposed to be going together."

126

George was starting to run out of arguments, but the change in Dave's story confirmed that he definitely didn't want George to go inside the apartment. He had to verify if Lisa was inside or not.

"Okay I won't push anymore then, oh well. However, can I just use your bathroom really quickly before I leave? I can't wait any longer, I've been walking for quite a long time to get here."

Dave closed the door a bit more and took on colder demeanor.

"No. You can't, it's clogged, the plumber was supposed to come today, but you know what it's like…"

"That's unfortunate, no luck, I guess. We'll I'll head off and leave you to finish getting ready, I'll find a public restroom and worst-case scenario, I'll go grab a drink in a bar assuming their toilets aren't clogged up too."

Lisa, laid out on the bed, began to come out of her haze slowly. She heard two voices mumbling from afar. She couldn't move her feet or her hands. Her mouth was dry, and her lips stuck together. She opened one eye carefully, and then the other. Her feet were attached with packing tape, and her hands were attached behind her back. Her mouth was also covered with the same tape.

She was still not fully recovered, but seeing the tape made her come to her senses much more quickly and a feeling of panic rolled down her spine. She listened more closely to the voices and she thought she could recognize those of Dave and George. For a moment she thought her mind was playing a trick on her, but it was definitely them. What was George doing here? How did he find her? She didn't understand anything, but the responses to her questions weren't important now. She tried to scream as loudly as she could with the tape covering her mouth, and she began to try and move around on the bed so that her feet would land on the carpet allowing her to stomp on the ground as hard as she could.

The noise didn't go unnoticed in the room next door. Dave tensed up as George was just turning to leave. George forced the door open and surprised Dave who was forced back as George entered the room. He hadn't had the chance to reach the door handle before Dave had taken a bronze statue and tried to aim for his head, but he missed his target and George was still advancing toward the bedroom door. He was able to strike George's back. The impact was violent, George fell forward and, his head knocked into the living room table, his inanimate body fell flat to the ground. His voice, twisted by hatred, uttered for the umpteenth time:

"She's *my* Lisa!"

**

The Commissioner walked briskly through the city's streets. Without hesitation or second-guessing, he navigated in the direction of Dave's apartment building. He arrived at the building's entrance. Strangely, the door was open. He climbed the stairs up to the second floor without bothering to buzz downstairs.

Once he arrived on the landing, he saw that the exact door he was looking for was hanging half open, which seemed strangers still. He slowly walked across the corridor. He heard sounds of a struggle taking place. He pushed the door open carefully, took one step inside and saw a man with a bronze statue in his hand, and another man laid out on the ground.

"Police!" he yelled. "Lower your weapon!"

But the man didn't seem to want to obey, he kept the statue, raised above his head and prepared to strike the fallen man another time. The Commissioner didn't leave him the time to complete the action, he threw himself onto the assailant, pushed him backwards and pinned him to the ground.

He looked around the room quickly to find something which he could use to subdue the man and tye his hands. He grabbed a scarf from underneath the couch and firmly tied Dave's hands together.

Then he took his phone out of his pocket and called the station for back-up.

George, still groggy, moved slightly.

"Are you okay, still with us?" Asked the Commissioner.

"Y-yeah. My head…" responded George, rolling onto his side and wincing at the pain.

"Stay where you are, don't move too much! An ambulance is on its way here."

"Lisa…" he mumbled, "Lisa...she's right there…" Then he fell, dazed.

George was once again unconscious. The Commissioner would take care of him after, the paramedics weren't that far away, and the priority now was to go and save Lisa.

E n d

Paul Beccaria

Epilogue

It had been more than an hour since George and Lisa first sat down at their table at Trattoria Toscana, just a few meters from the Dome of Milan. This edifice, the pride of the people who had sacrificed themselves for the decades it took to build it, maintained its poise now while faced with hordes of tourists and artists who had come to admire it and the artists that came by daily and set up to paint its likeness.

With both hands, George took Lisa's right and placed a gentle kiss upon it.

"Andrew, gather your toys, we'll be leaving soon."

The little boy raised his big eyes to meet Lisa's and began to pout as though preparing to throw a fit, but he held back. He opted for a simple sigh and shook his little brown curls with a resigned air.

"Okay, fine mama."

Homage

"I loved God, who is nothing in the eyes of men who are nothing. I hated neither man nor woman. And I loved life, which is far less than nothing, but is everything to us."

-      Jean d'Ormesson

Comme un chant d'espérance

(Like A Song of Hope)

www.ingramcontent.com/pod-product-compliance
Lightning Source LLC
Chambersburg PA
CBHW021923170626
46807CB00007B/2963